COWS!

Published by Fishcakes Publications

www.fishcakepublications.com

71 Royds Avenue, Linthwaite, Huddersfield, HD7 5SA

ISBN 978-1-909015-02-9

© **Martin D Rothery 2013.**

Previously published in March 2012

Second Edition Published in Great Britain in 2013.

Cover Illustrations by Martin Rothery.

Cover arrangement in collaboration with Warren Lee.

Dedicated to my beloved Clare,

my family and my friends at HWG.

Thank-you for your support.

Contents

Before It Begins...

"Has an emissary been located?"

"We have identified an infant human male in the nearby village who has the correct genetic DNA sequencing that we have been searching for. In our opinion he is a perfect match."

"Really? A perfect match? We couldn't have hoped for better. Training and conditioning needs to begin immediately."

"I've already instructed our top agents to begin the task."

"Good. The sooner the tempering begins the more effective he will be in the future. What about a guardian, has a suitable candidate been found?"

"Scouts report healthy specimens on the local farm, born of excellent herding stock. We have worked with the mother and father on several occasions and believe they will be more than cooperative. They are sympathetic to the cause."

"This is most fortuitous. Advise them of the situation and see which candidate they recommend for advancement. Secrecy is of paramount importance as you already know. Discretion is a priority."

"Of course. But may I also advise caution. This is a bold plan, not to mention dangerous should the enemy find out. Are you sure we can implement it effectively?"

"We have been left with no choice. We know they have begun to formulate new plans; we must have a counter offensive prepared, even if we don't need to use it. Our statisticians predict they will be ready to act in approximately twelve to fourteen years time. We must be ready to act."

"It shall be done."

COWS!

"Good, now will you move your hooves and get off that piece of grass – it looks delicious and I'm starving."

Chapter 1

Chew, Chew, Chew.

When you watch a cow in a field you don't expect to see very much happen do you, just *chew, chew, chew.*

Maybe you'll get a *moo.*

Chew, Chew, Chew.

Moo, Moo, Moo.

That would seem to be pretty much it!

Therefore it may come as some surprise to you that behind those big black docile eyes with their merrily fluttering eyelashes lurk some of the keenest minds you'll ever encounter on planet earth.

Yes, really!

And they are planning to take over the world!

Does that come as something of a shock to you?

Let me explain.

You see, they're smarter than those cuddly little chimps who, to their credit, may be beginning to develop the use of rudimentary tools or those cocky dolphins who perform for the public in exchange for rewards of fishy treats. Their intelligence pales in comparison to these grass eating methane generators that dwell in our countryside much closer to home.

For reasons that will soon become apparent, they just don't want us to know!

Of course, there are sheep in the country as well – and they know. They've always known. We just didn't know that they know because they didn't want us to know.

COWS!

It's one big countryside conspiracy – humans not included.

It may surprise you that, in this surreal world of countryside intrigue, that we do have some farmyard allies, notably in the form of pigs. They are very fond of humans, but if they told us what was going on, they'd be considered squealers.

To begin this tale of farmyard conspiracy, let me take you to a small country village, nestling among the lush green valleys of the Yorkshire hills. A quiet, sleepy, yet spirited community built on the traditions of farming and priding itself on its dairy herds.

Come to think of it, they are rather strangely devoted to these undisclosed Bovine masterminds, bordering on fanaticism almost. What better place to start a revolution.

We join our black and white meaty renegades at their daily strategic, analytical, tactical, planning, territorial campaign meeting – also known as milking time.

Within the earthy smelling, dimly lit confines of the milking shed, the air thick and heavy, we find our Bovine aggressors conspiring amongst the background hum and gurgling of the machinery, many of them lazily chewing the fodder as they have their udders evacuated, occasionally bellowing out a moo or a grunt. At a brief glance to the passing observer, nothing would really look out of the ordinary. But don't be fooled, they are the masters of deception.

"I call this meeting to order!" bellowed the Prime Admiral Tactical Commander of Herd (codenamed

P.A.T.C.H and quite appropriate really due to her unusual marking that has the familiarity of a quilt knitted by your favourite Granny).

Patch was a tyrant among her kind, who commanded obedience and definitely stood out among the herd.

She was also the leader because she was the biggest!

Often leading by example, this trooper was known to eat up to two hundred pounds of grass and drink one hundred gallons of water in a day which was phenomenal for a cow, roughly twice the daily amount required, an inspiring precedent for all her troop. Why you may ask? Well, imagine the output from the other end, something that all cows aim for and would be explained soon enough.

Although the cows were having a meeting, we *know* they can't actually talk, not in the conventional sense anyway. If this was the case then surely they would have given themselves away a long time ago and we would have cottoned on that they were up to something. Can you imagine the publicity of a talking cow! By jingo, that would never do; they needed to be discreet in their affairs.

The mooing mellowed down to a low background throb of rumbles, snorts and gurgles with a few rump trumpets thrown in.

"Ooooh, the farmer's put the suction up too high again," groaned Delta Alpha 1 5 Yankee (conveniently codenamed D.A.1.5.Y), "the tubes are really chafing my udders." Her knees were knocking together like coconuts on a palm in a force five gale. She was trembling so much the black and white hide had blended into grey.

"*Thank-you*, for that amazing insight Daisy." Patch shot the cause of the interruption a big black-eyed look of disapproval. "You've got no-one to blame but yourself. If you'd been concentrating on the human instead of idly tit-tattling to your buddies when you came in, you could have instructed *it* to lower the pressure. Let that lapse be a lesson to you! The humans are ours to command but you have to stay focused at all times."

The surprising use of cow telepathy allowed them to keep their thoughts to themselves, and each other, another hidden truth behind Bovine advanced culture that has developed over the millennia.

However, many cow theologians philosophise it may have been better to evolve the ability to milk themselves which would be a much more useful skill to their species as humans (or calf birth) were still required to remove their milk.

If they weren't milked, it could be quite uncomfortable and unpleasant for a cow resulting in the need for dirty human medical attention – *or worse!*

"Sorry Ma'am. It won't happen again." Shifting uncomfortably, Daisy started counting the grains in the trough before her, avoiding eye contact with her immediate counterparts.

These meeting were held every day and were orchestrated by Patch to be used to discuss tactical deployment, distribution, human domination and, of course, where the best grass was.

"Today's meeting is very important!" Patch announced to the gathered herd. Our numerous years of planning, work and toil are about to come to fruition. I've received word from H.E.R.D command and they believe we have reached a critical juncture in which to advance our plans and more excitingly our unit has been chosen by the High Longhorn herself, *long live her Hornness," this was echoed throughout the shed,* " to undertake an advance mission to seek any signs of resistance prior to full deployment."

The 'Human and Earth Radical Domination' command is the Bovine agency in charge of taking over the planet. It is believed to be based in Devon, which makes sense as they are the cream of the crop, but this has never been confirmed

"Ooooh, how exciting a secret mission. I'm so nervous it's making my rump tingle!"

Patch's eyes narrowed as she, once again, stared through the gloom at the source of constant interruptions.

"Thank-you *again* Daisy for another *remarkable* comment that once again *emphasizes* the *importance* of this unique mission," Patch said demonstrating the Bovine legendary sarcasm. In fact to say a cow wasn't sarcastic would be like saying milk isn't white and doesn't make yoghurt. (That's the traditional stuff of course with no fancy fruit purees or distracting chocolaty sprinkles packaged in unnecessary compartmentalized plastic cornered container); "anyhow…..I have orders to begin 'Operation Milkshake'."

A few shifting hooves of nervousness around the room as well as a few involuntary oscillating releases of methane from rear ends; the most obvious sense of tension releasing.

"This is due to commence at 0600 hours – milking time tomorrow. I'm now going to hand over to the Command Liaison Officer Vanguard Enforcement Registrar for further details and instructions." She's known as C.L.O.V.E.R to you and me, otherwise that would be quite a mouthful, wouldn't it?

Quite incidentally, she had a black Patch on her shoulder that did actually resemble a four leaf Clover. Ironically, it never brought her any luck.

Cow's names are frequently abbreviated and become very similar to the fondly given pet names we may give a cow? Quite a nice coincidence isn't it? It makes them sound a little nicer and easier to relate to for humans. Shame they wish to force total dominion over us. You never know, on another planet, at another time we may have even been friends; but no point in philosophising over that now.

"Thank-you Ma'am." Clover enthusiastically lolled forward to the head of the cow shed before being promptly catapulted back in surprise after forgetting she still had the suction tubes attached to her udders.

She promptly got back up and blew the straw out of her nose, unconvincingly trying to look as casual and dignified under the circumstances as she came forward again, more tentatively this time. Cows don't blush and go red like humans do; however the milk that was being sucked out of her began resembling a strawberry milkshake.

"As you know, this unit has been doing some excellent work in collaboration with other local and regional units. Our herd's methane production alone has helped raise the planet's temperature by one tenth of a degree Celsius, a fabulous achievement I'm sure you'll agree. This greenhouse gas effect is having the predicted results in raising the planet's ambient temperature and is now at the optimum level for maximum telepathic yield. The funny thing is, and I'm sure you'll agree, is that we still have the humans believing that it is them causing the phenomenon by burning their fossil fuels, ha ha."

Her chuckles were echoed around the room.

What is all that about I hear you asking? This all sounds like Gobble-De-Gook (although the feathered future Christmas dinners, known as Turkeys, would prefer the term Gobble-De-Gobble as they can't say Gook).

It's no secret that scientists have recently discovered the amount of gaseous discharge coming from the Bovine community has been contributing to global warming.

The third largest contributor in the world, apparently.

Little did they know it was deliberate.

You see, cows like a warm environment, there's no doubting that. The problem with Old Blighty is the temperature for most of the year is, let's face it, pretty cold and this can lead to very inactive cows. You'll probably agree, during most of the time throughout the year you'll see them standing around in fields fairly statuesque. This is how they get caught by those terrible cow-tippers. Many a Friesian has ended up on its side after these pranksters had sneaked up on them and pushed them over, just for a laugh. This is not amusing to the poor cow, who just didn't have the energy to move away.

Most of the time, they can just about manage to chew, but in our climate this takes tremendous concentration and effort.

In comparison, on a warm summer's day, this can be their most productive time. If you were to venture in to the countryside and stand amongst a herd for a while, being both very still and quiet, the most common noise you would hear is an orchestral fanfare of raspberry style eruptions.

So now we know they are trying to warm the planet, why is that you may ask?

Let's find out more from Clover.

"The mean ambient global temperature has now reached critical density for optimal telepathic discharge to be transmitted allowing full mental assault upon the human species. Lactose cerebral control formulation has reached maximum yield resulting in optimum consumption and Homosapian saturation to allow remote brain operation."

"Do you mean the humans have drunk enough milk changing their brain chemistry and now the air is warm enough for us to use our brainwaves to control their tiny little minds?" enquired a confused looking Daisy.

"Yes Daisy, I thought that's what I said?" Clover rolled her eyes.

"Oh….. good." Daisy slowly nodded as it all began to register.

Patch moved back to the fore.

"As you know, we've been planning this takeover for some time now. Our ancestors conceived this plan decades ago and it has taken some time to reach this critical juncture. We will make them proud. For too long, too many of our kind have been made into roast dinners and beef burgers. Tomorrow, we will honour their sacrifice!" Patch's rallying cry raised moos of approval; "We will take control of the humans and bind them to us as our slaves. Tomorrow, we take this village, after that we will become rulers of the world!"

This dramatic speech was met with rousing applause, or more accurately, a large stomping of hooves.

Well, that sounds exciting and dramatic doesn't it? But let's just take time to remember, cows can't actually speak English. Of course they can't. They don't have the ability to move tongues and lips as we do, not to mention the fact they don't have a voice box. And besides, who would teach them? They can't exactly walk into a primary school and ask someone to teach them their a, b, c's can they? Cows can't read our language either.

However, taking this into account, it wouldn't make a very interesting story if we couldn't understand what they were saying would it? So, I have taken the time to translate for you. This was not an easy feat, mind. Cow is no easy language to learn, so the translation may not be one hundred percent accurate. I still have trouble with pre-tensed double hyphenated moo come rumble that is deep from the back of the throat. Be warned, if translated incorrectly it could refer to some rather rude insult towards your parentage. (Just try it; you'll see what I mean.)

The meeting continued late into the evening, the final elements of the plan being finely honed and polished, and up above the sun set over the old wooden cowshed hitting the atmosphere with its amber glow.

Down in the nearby valley, in the village of Golthwaite, lights began appearing in the little cottage windows deterring the ingress of night. Peaceful, nocturnal activities began oblivious to the fortunes that lay ahead for the inhabitants within.

In The Meantime...

"Latest intelligence reports they are due to commence their offensive."

"What? They must be mad! Do they not realise if they commence these actions then the treaty is broken?"

"Affirmative. They must be confident in their plan if they are willing to risk a peace that has lasted this long."

"The problem is we don't know the full extents of their plan. We need more information. Is the Avian spy network in position?"

"Yes, they are on constant alert and currently active. Reports are starting to come in but we have nothing concrete as yet."

"Is the emissary prepared and up to the task?"

"Training and conditioning has taken place over the last ten years. Although his general intelligence quotient is below normal level, his aptitude, empathy, cognitive skills and competence rate very highly."

"He still remains unaware of our interaction but this will allow him to fulfil his task more efficiently without directly implementing ourselves. Unfortunately, some side effects have become apparent, but these are negligible"

"Good. From all other reports the guardian is also doing an excellent job and has firmly bonded with the emissary. She still shows some signs of resistance to us but this is no more than a slight rebellious streak within her."

"Will she be responsive should the task require her skills?"

"Yes, she is more than ready and should the need arise, she will seek our aid."

"Good. Also, order the Avians to render any aid or warning where necessary."

"We are now on full alert – as soon as I've had a nibble on that delicious looking clover over there".

Chapter 2

As the evening drifts in over the little village of Golthwaite, we join one of its junior inhabitants safely residing in one of the beautiful little stone cottages that bordered the village green.

This certain young lad, Jimmy Tatley was his name, was readying himself for bed even though it was only just turning eight o'clock. You may think this is a little bit soon for a bed time, especially as this young man was fourteen and he could stay up until at least half past ten if he wanted to. His parents, Gerald and Susan Tatley, wouldn't have minded, as even they thought it was a bit weird for a lad his age to be putting his head down early. There had never been any sign of teenage rebellion in him.

Laid at the bottom of his bed, watching his every move with disinterest, was a black and white border collie.

"Ok Flossy, my alarm is set; my wellies are ready by the door with your collar and lead…" Flossy lifted her head and looked up at Jimmy judgingly; he caught the glare in her eye. "…alright, we'll not take your lead; I know you don't like it." Flossy settled her head back down between her front paws, seemingly pacified.

"Where's my whistle? Oh, there it is. Can't do with forgetting that can we, otherwise you'll be pretending not to hear me again at sheep herding practice, won't you lass."

Now, as you know, dogs can't speak English, but they do understand it and human folk perfectly well, so she did what she did best and pretended to ignore him (just like when he kept blowing that irritating whistle). Although she loved her owner, and they had a very strong bond, he did wind her up sometimes.

"We'll get up nice and early tomorrow lass; about quarter past four should do it. I told Farmer Ken I'd be at the farm around five-ish to help get the cows in for milking."

Tomorrow was Saturday and Jimmy loved Saturdays as he got to help out on the local farm, just on the outskirts of the village, which was owned by Farmer Ken.

It had turned out that Jimmy had a natural talent with all animals, an unusual empathy that allowed easy collaboration and understanding with them on an unseen level; all except cows. Strangely enough there always seemed to be an innate sense of distrust with them.

He was also not afraid of hard work and getting his hands dirty – what better place to apply these talents than on a farm.

To be fair Jimmy wasn't the brightest of lads. At school he struggled with his a, b, d's, thought geometry was a form of earth measuring and home economics was the art of mathematics practiced by estate agents. He was never going to be an extraordinary academic. Therefore he and his parents were delighted to find he had such a knack with animals and he had taken to farming as a goose takes to a pond.

Farmer Ken was a friend of Jimmy's father (as was everyone else who went drinking down at the Frog on the Green public house on a Friday night), so Gerald had asked him if Jimmy could spend the odd Saturday helping out on the local farm and to Jimmy's delight and good luck, he'd agreed. (Actually there wasn't much luck involved as Farmer Ken, being a tight fisted skinflint, was never going to turn down free labour).

Therefore every Friday night you would find Jimmy getting ready for bed early, brimming with excitement, so he could be up and off at first light.

He stripped off his woolly slippers, pulled on his slightly faded navy blue woollen pyjamas, slid himself under his soft, cosy woollen sheets and put his messy brown haired head down on fluffy woollen pillow whilst cuddling his woolly stuffed toy sheep.

I know what you're thinking – that sounds like a lot of wool. You see, Jimmy loved wool but could never explain to anyone why. He just felt so comfortable either in it, on it or surrounded by it. A bit unusual you might think and you'd probably be right. It was even bordering on obsession. Even on a hot sunny day, you'd find Jimmy wearing his woolly pullover. He'd even named his sheepdog Flossy (a name she was not at all happy with at all, when the last thing she needed was a constant reminder of the role that had been dictated to her within canine society. The thought of even chasing sheep made her tired and she blatantly refused to count them just to get to sleep. She was pretty sure she could turn her talents to other uses. But obviously, she couldn't tell him all of this, she was only a dog!

"Goodnight Flossy, sleep tight girl, busy day tomorrow."

If only he had known how busy it was going to be.

Jimmy was awake before the alarm even sounded. The young lad contentedly lay snug, wrapped in his woolly covers coming around as he slowly waited for the monotonous chimes to begin. There was a slight chill in the air and the sunlight was already beginning to intrude between the cracks in the curtains promising a grand day ahead. Flossy was curled up the foot of Jimmy's bed still fast asleep in an attempt to try and delay the day ahead.

The alarm heralded the time to rise and, startled, Flossy jumped and fell off the bed in a great heap. Heaving himself slowly out from under his blanket he bent down and lifted the big shaggy pile of black and white fur off the floor, placed her gently back on the bed and gave her an affectionate tickle behind the ears.

"Come on girl, time to get up. Let's get dressed, get some brekkie and then we can be off." She did not look too enthusiastic and began the dreaded wait till they had to leave.

Stretching off the morning grogginess he began to pull on his clothes, all wool of course, even, rather strangely, his underpants. Once dressed Jimmy wandered over to the window and pulled back the curtains, soaking himself in the early morning sun that streamed in, it was going to be a lovely day. Wide awake now, he quietly opened his door, left his room, crept his way across the landing and then downstairs on his tippy toes.

The house was as silent as a stone, which was to be expected at around four thirty in the morning as his parents were still in bed fast asleep, but for Jimmy something didn't feel quite right. As his ears strained he realised that he couldn't hear the usual unearthly rattle that was his father's snoring. Normally at this time it would be shaking the tiles on the roof but today there was not as much as a whispering snort to be heard.

"I'll bet mum has stuffed a sock in his mouth, Flossy," Jimmy whispered in a grin as she padded along beside him. "She's been threatening to do it all this time; sounds like she's finally done it." He chuckled to himself as he continued his toe ended descent.

He hastily made himself some toast, downed a glass of orange juice and put a bowl of food down, absently dispensed from the first can he found, for Flossy who, unseen to Jimmy, looked at his back with disapproval and disgust with the choice put before her. Unsurprisingly the dog food he had given her was lamb. She would have chosen anything but and considered if sometimes he did it on purpose.

Breakfast out of the way, Jimmy enthusiastically pulled on his wellies, slipped the wool collar on Flossy (remembering to leave the lead to one side), grabbed his woolly coat, checked his pocket for his dog whistle and then was swiftly but silently exiting through the kitchen door, meandering down the cobble path through the beautifully manicured front garden to the gleaming white wooden gate. Heading through, he carefully closed it behind him and pointed himself down the lane in the direction of Farmer Ken's farm.

Now most Saturday mornings, most normal places that you and I may come from are usually quiet at such an ungodly time of the morning. At the end of a working week we all like a bit of a lie in to recharge our batteries and so on. Therefore you really wouldn't expect to see many people around and about in the small hours of Saturday morning and as Jimmy made his way through the quaint village streets, bordered by grass verges, tidily manicured hedgerows and neatly laid drystone walls bordering the villagers' ordered and blossoming gardens, they were unsurprisingly deserted.

Unsurprising to you or me that is because as mentioned before, this was a village built on farming tradition. Early mornings were part of everyday life here so you would usually find at least one or two of the native folk on their way to work or maybe a few lights in windows as people breakfasted.

But - there was no-one.

Nothing moved.

Jimmy thought there was something wrong with his ears and shoved his index finger deep in his right one just to test it was working. He was rewarded with a waxy fingertip.

If it wasn't for the slight rustling of the leaves as the breeze gently nudged them into movement or the sound of his own footsteps on the path, he could have sworn he had lost his hearing.

Where were the paperboys doing their morning deliveries? Where were the market traders who would normally be setting up their stalls on the village green and the farmers bringing their wares to be traded? But most importantly where was the wool stall that regularly drew Jimmy's attention like a big fluffy magnet. He couldn't help it; the colour, texture and variety seemed to just grab his attention. Jimmy was often asked by Mrs Shearing, the stall owner, to move along as the drooling Jimmy often scared her customers as well as rendered her stock rather damp

It was only then that Jimmy noticed the birds, but not in the usual sense. They were flying around, whizzing across the sky in the normal manner doing what birds do best – either tree hopping, collecting nest materials or scrabbling around on the ground digging for worms, berries and seeds – but he couldn't hear them.

However, their eyes were always intent on what was going on upon the ground as if watching for something.

But, they were all silent, no noise passed their beaks.

Where was the dawn chorus?

You may or may not agree, but one of the most pleasant experiences to be had in the country is to wake up in bed and listen to the bird song permeate the morning air – it warms the heart. After a while it becomes an unnoticed background noise but it still provides an omnipotent symphony that fills the countryside with avian melody

Jimmy felt strangely uneasy; with every step he thought he would shatter the very air with every thud of his feet. Each breath seemed to be stretching the atmosphere with its rasping.

Then something peculiar happened.

In the periphery of his vision, Jimmy spotted a small blur hurtling from the sky and landing just ahead of him before suddenly realising what it was. "Well hello Mr. Robin, why aren't you tweeting this morning?"

The robin sat about three metres away from Jimmy on a garden spade handle, (because that's usually where you usually find a robin of course as they do seem strangely drawn to them), where it was tilting its head giving the young lad a curious but appraising look. The questioning in its eyes seemed to suggest misunderstanding, almost as if Jimmy shouldn't be there. This made Jimmy shiver rather uncomfortably.

"Tweet-Tware," the little brown and red feathered bundle emitted.

Wide eyed, Jimmy gaped before replying..."Err...What?" It's amazing how articulate he could be sometimes!

"Tweet-Tware, Tsutid."

It appeared to be conversing with him. Jimmy was stunned beyond belief.

This really comes as no surprise at all when you think about it as robins know all about us. They are nosy so and so's. You'll catch them looking in through your window, or sitting on a post nearby, seemingly innocent, but all the time they are actually spying on us. Just you have a look next time you see one.

"Er…what?" he repeated in the absence of any other words forming due to the shocking developments.

The robin's expression took on a disgruntled appearance and it let out a sigh that seemed slightly larger than one it should be able to produce for something of its size. It hopped down on to the dirty path and began scratching along the ground with its beak.

Jimmy's face beamed with delight at this spectacle watching this fascinating feathered artist in action as Flossy looked on unimpressed – show off she thought. It all looked like a lot of effort to her.

B….E….W….A….R….E.

The young lad looked at the letters scrawled in the earth.

"I get the feeling it's trying to tell us something Flossy, what could it be?"

Flossy lay down on her belly, lowered her head and put her paws over her face letting out a small moan. The robin shrugged its wings.

C….O….W….S.

The robin looked up at the boy; agitatedly hopping around the letters it had just scribed upon the floor hoping enlightenment may suddenly dawn upon him.

Unfortunately, if Jimmy's brain was a hotel then his eyes would have been displaying the vacant sign.

"I'm sorry Mr. Robin but I don't have time to play hangman, I have to go to work; maybe another time though," and with that Jimmy turned away shaking his head. "C'mon Flossy we'll be late."

Trouble is Jimmy had the tendency to get bored a little too easily with things he didn't really understand. Plus he had the attention span of a cat in a string factory; not a good combination. So as he continued along the picturesque country lane, becoming distracted by a beautiful display of yellow and pink flowers that were trailing over the drystone wall of Mrs. Pettigrew's garden, he was soon forgetting about the tiny Avian and its cryptic message.

The robin, after all its hard work, was not amused.

"Twit!" chirped the fiery chested bird whose torso appeared to have gone an even angrier shade of red than before and was hopping on the spot shaking its little feathery head, a tiny swirl of dust forming at its feet.

"Oh yes, Twit Twit," Jimmy caught himself replying and turned waving goodbye. Smiling to himself he said, "What a lovely little creature."

Looking back, out of Jimmy's sight, Flossy eyed the robin suspiciously through squinted eyes. She was quite intelligent and knew something was going on; that this Avian's warning should be heeded. She almost felt embarrassed that her owner could dismiss such an obvious sign; then again maybe that's why she was around. Although he didn't know it, they made a good pair and more often than not she would get Jimmy out of all sorts of precarious situations.

She glanced back at the robin and gave it a sly nod and a wink whilst the teenagers back was turned, a sign of understanding between the two. In return the bird opened its wings wide and lifted its eyes to the sky, almost deflating as it let out a huge breath, a distinct sign of relief that someone had understood the message.

A few minutes later they were passing through the large flaky green painted planks of wood that made up the big farm gate. Their rickety construction belied the weight of these timber barriers which Jimmy, even for a strapping young lad, normally struggled to move on his own. Normally he would climb over them, it was much easier. Lying wide open as they were now however worried Jimmy slightly as Farmer Ken liked to keep them closed at all times just in case any of the animals got loose. The proprietor was usually very particular and meticulous about details like this.

In addition to this the farm was quiet – too quiet.

No cockerels crowing.

No sheep bleating.

No pigs squealing.

No cows mooing.

Of course, where were the cows?

It was milking time and, looking around at the surrounding fields, they were nowhere to be seen. Around now, they would be normally waiting at the gate at the end of the lane that entered the field where they grazed and they knew they were going to be fed and milked. They weren't there and the gate was wide open.

Jimmy's thought (he could only form one at a time, poor lad,) immediately turned to Farmer Ken.

"I think something odd's going on here Flossy, things just don't seem right. We have to find Farmer Ken and make sure he's ok. We'll go to the farmhouse first, maybe he's just having a late breakfast. You never know if we're lucky, Mrs. Farmer Ken…" (She preferred to be called Nishitori or Nishi to her friends, but Jimmy was always respectful) "…might have some bacon and egg kung po waiting for us." Nishi's stir fry's were legendary and Flossy's ears pricked up at this tit bit of information, she preferred pork to lamb any day.

They continued to make their way along the winding pebble path, passing the stone sculptures, lotus blossoms, bonsai and stunning purple acer trees, crunching their way through the still present silence, towards what can only be described as a chocolate box, picture postcard perfect farmyard cottage.

Farmer Ken kept it in immaculate condition inside and out from the perfect stone tiled roof to the beautifully white painted cottage windows set neatly between the fine quarried stone blocks that had stood against the ravages of time. The whole front façade was softened by the green ivy waterfall that cascaded from the roof to the garden below. The path led right up to a wonderfully inviting wooden front door framed by an ornate Japanese style pergola covered in pink trailing roses.

However this was all lost on Jimmy who, following the lead of his ever ravenous belly skirted his way around towards the back of the cottage towards the back door as this was the fastest access to the kitchen. He was rounding the last corner when...

They just stood there.

Tens of black glass marbles set into long snouted black and white visages all staring at him. Jimmy froze.

They didn't move.

Jimmy didn't move.

They stared at him.

He stared back.

Their long Bovine faces showed no emotion (nothing new there).

Jimmy's face rarely showed any kind of emotion at all as this required complex thinking and coordination but on this occasion a slight frown seemed to appear on his brow.

The intensity of that collective glare penetrated right through him, almost as if they were trying to find something deep within his body, within his mind. You could argue they would be lucky to find anything of value within that brain of his anyway but they seemed intent upon finding something.

At the front of the herd was a larger cow with a checkerboard patchwork appearance who was getting very annoyed as well as slightly confused – why wasn't this boy responding to her mind probes? The blank vacant expression of this human boy's face suggested that their mental assault was working but the weird thing was she just couldn't register any control, activity or consciousness at all come to think of it, within his head. Surely this youth couldn't be brain dead: there had been no zombie activity reported for years. She seriously couldn't believe this backward little village community had enough collective intelligence within it to construct an android – of course not; he couldn't be one of those. It had taken her years to design of them herself and her intelligence was vastly superior; even though her mighty intellect hadn't succumbed to the common sense notion that she would never be able to build it having no articulate hands to manage the feat. She mentally reminded herself that she would have to get one of her future human slaves to build it for her.

She put aside and discounted the zombie and android options and turned her mind back to the current task that presented itself.

The staring had now been going on for several minutes and neither party looked like giving way at any point. This made Flossy a little uneasy. She kept turning her head from the group to her master for signs of…well anything, but both the cows and Jimmy were as statues locked in a battle of *dim*wits.

The cows appeared frozen in the pose of being caught doing something they shouldn't have been - like rabbits caught in the headlights, (although rabbits usually prefer spotlights. They are excellent performers and are a boon at any talent contest or gala. It was the rabbits that taught the magicians to pull them out of the hat and not the other way around, you know), and Jimmy simply appeared dumbstruck at the appearance of the cows in the back yard.

Emitting a low growl, Flossy began to nudge Jimmy just behind the knee.

"Wha…Oh, not now girl. I'm having a staring competition with these cows – and I think I'm winning."

Flossy's eyes rolled. She grabbed the top of his welly in her teeth and gave a sharp tug, putting Jimmy off balance. The eye contact was lost as he stumbled slightly and tried to regain his pose.

"Flossy! Oh, ok. I suppose you're right. I'll never beat a cow at this game, they are so dumb. I think we better find Farmer Ken and tell him the cows are loose in his back yard. He'll want them back in the shed for milking and not idling about playing silly games with us."

Innocently, he turned his back on the cows and set off back around the cottage heading for the front door instead as they were blocking the access to the rear kitchen door and there was no way he would be able to move them.

Flossy, on the other hand, backed up tentatively never taking her eyes off the black and white barrier.

Just as he was rounding the corner of the building, Jimmy quickly glanced back peeping around the gable end to see if they were still there. Those shiny black orbs were still peering back...

"I'll beat you next time," was his parting shot.

"Why couldn't we control him?" Patch angrily shot the accusation at Clover.

"I...err...I mean...I don't know, I'm at a complete loss Ma'am. I could register no brain activity or consciousness there at all. It was almost as if he wasn't there."

"I sensed the very same thing. This is not good. That human has the potential to harm our plans. We must put an elite detachment on him now and discover how he is resisting us. I want that boy hunted down. Daisy, front and centre!"

"Yes Ma'am!" Daisy was before her leader faster than they could recite the Bovine national anthem, which incidentally has over one hundred verses mainly about grass and how to chew it, so you can imagine her speed.

"Track that human youth and his mangy canine. Find out what he is up to – detain him if possible, use force if necessary, but don't kill him. I need to run some tests to find out how he has just resisted us. Take as many troops as you need. Now go."

"Yes Ma'am. Buttercup, Dandelion, Hyacinth – you're with me."

(If I even tried to decipher all those code aliases it would take ages and I'm sure you would rather get on with the story instead.)

Daisy, although sometimes a little scatterbrained for a mentally acute cow, was actually an elite commander of a sub-unit within the herd known as the 'Cowssassins'.

As you would expect from the name, they are considered quite dangerous and unbelievably they are armed with over one hundred ways to kill. Luckily these skills are rarely used on humans. Their most obvious tactic they employ is the stampede, a favourite amongst the Spanish and American herds (you must have seen the chases in the Iberian streets or the old Wild West films – they were all planned by cows). However, in Old Blighty, these cows prefer the more traditional approach of sitting on a victim until they passed out or suffocated and cleverly making it look like an accident. Well how many people would believe a cow fell or sat on a human on purpose? This is considered a more refined and civilised approach in cow society as opposed the brash approach of their foreign cousins.

Daisy and her elite quad shot into action, moving with the speed, grace and elegance of drunken jelly. Loping in the same direction as Jimmy, faster than speeding custard.

Of course, if Jimmy had known about this, he could have sat down, had a glass of lemonade, got up casually and strolled away without a care in the world. He was totally oblivious to any danger that would befall him. As far as he was concerned they were just silly cows.

Meanwhile to the rear of the farmhouse the anger expressed by Patch at this moment made her go redder and redder. Her appearance was now more of a giant ladybird than that of a cow.

"Why couldn't I probe his mind? When I focused on his head, it was empty"

Jimmy's teachers had suspected that for years but never had the telepathic ability to prove it.

If world domination was going to be realised every human had to be under their mental influence. That might be difficult if some of them didn't contain a brain.

Patch re-capped the plan in her own calculative, brilliant and devious mind with an IQ in human terms of ten thousand and three. She'd added on four points herself, just because she was being overly clever and didn't like numbers all containing the same numeral. Nine thousand, nine hundred and ninety nine was so cliché in cow circles, so she added on her number of legs just for fun.

Going though every detail, Patch thought she'd covered every angle, so this anomaly was beginning to vex her.

Schematics of her invention, the Quasispectrographic-magnomatrix-homospaieninterphasic-mechanelectrolosisagram (or human DNA scanner for Bovine kind) whizzed through her mind and the results of all the tests had proved positive when tested on the humans. All subjects had proved susceptible to milk telepathic saturation influences when she had scanned them.

So why was this young lad such an anomaly?

Her hunters would bring him in and she would find out.

And, she thought to herself, she would have won that staring contest if it wasn't for that pesky mutt.

Whilst All This Is Going On...

"Latest intelligence reports the Bovines are beginning to mobilise. The farming staff has been incapacitated."

"And so it begins. We knew that they were planning but the speed of deployment has found us unprepared. What reports do we have from the village?"

"Bovine squads are being deployed in strategic positions allowing them use telepathy to maximum effect. We believe ninety nine percent of the village population are now under their influence, but this is rising as we speak."

"They are keeping the humans immobile for now but it only a matter of time before they animate them for their own purposes."

"How fares the emissary? Have we made contact with him yet?"

"One Avian agent has attempted to make contact with him to give warning but this had little effect. We believe the guardian may have interpreted the message however."

"Good. She's a smart girl and will act accordingly."

"The same agent reports after following him, that the emissary has made contact with the Bovines on the farm and has showed amazing signs of resistance. No effect at all, in fact. He has walked away from the confrontation unscathed leaving the Bovines in some confusion"

"That is excellent news. This will allow him to act on behalf of the humans although now they will be aware of his potential threat therefore putting him in immediate danger and they may move against him."

"Everyone stay alert. Keep the reports coming in and keep monitoring their progress. We must not let them succeed but we must wait for the right moment to act. I feel the emissary will need our aid in the near future."

"Now let me scratch in peace; I've been itching all over since I've been shaved and now I'm expecting some quality time with the trunk of a tree"

Chapter 3

The summer morning was beginning to take full effect by now and it looked like it would be a lovely sunny day. The temperature was warming up gradually and within it seemed to contain an unseen but perceptibly felt vibration in the air, as if buzzing with a static electricity just on the edge of touch. Of course, Jimmy didn't notice this but it was putting Flossy on edge, her heightened senses picking up the subtle changes in atmospheric pressure and electromagnetism. She didn't like it one bit and increased her alertness to her surroundings but made sure she kept Jimmy in sight at all times. There might be a moment when she was needed to guide and protect the young lad and she was making sure she was ready.

By now, Jimmy was knocking at the heavy oak stable style door at the front of the farmhouse, rapping loudly with the ornately decorated black wrought iron door-knocker forged into the shape of a samurai's helmet with an ugly face peering from within... The noise was enough to raise the recently interred, never mind the sleeping folk. There was no response from within though.

Gently trying the handle, "It's not locked, Flossy," Jimmy said as the old door squeaked open before sticking his head in through the crack and shouting out, "Farmer Ken! Mrs Farmer Ken! Are you here? It's Jimmy. Hello!"

There was no answer but his own echo.

Pushing the door fully open, he stepped through and entered into the hallway, Flossy close on his heels, then shut the door behind him just as a cow's face was beginning to appear around the side of the frame. More interested in searching the interior, he didn't notice it as he busily cast his eyes around the cottage for any sign of the farming couple.

Nor did he notice the muffled 'oomph' sound of the cow that had just had the door slammed on its nose.

It was eerily silent. The curtains were closed and there were no lights on so it took Jimmy a couple of moments for his eyes to adjust to his now dimly lit surroundings. He started tip-toeing around in cartoon style as not to make any loud noises on the stone flag floor, which seems a bit silly really as he was only shouting a few moments before.

Flossy casually plodded after him.

Turning to his left he opened a bamboo and paper screen door that separated the hall from the living room noticing as he entered that the blinds were still down over the windows in this room too. Jimmy crossed the floor in slow deliberate steps so as not to fall over the low table and seating cushions that were placed in the middle barely visible in the tricky half light that invaded around the edge of the blinds somehow mysteriously glinting on the samurai sword above the mantel piece. It was very neat, tidy and organised, which was to be expected of the Farmers Ken's, as they always ran a neat, tidy and tight ship.

Jimmy now found himself in front of the screen door to the kitchen but still there was no hint of life coming from beyond. Sliding aside the door and quietly entering he surveyed the situation before him. Unfortunately there was no sign of breakfast being made making both Jimmy's and Flossy's stomachs groan in disappointment.

"Weird, they must have slept in Flossy, that's not like them. Hope they're not ill or anything. C'mon let's go and wake them up. We need to get those cows into the shed quickly and we can't do it alone."

Luckily, Jimmy got on very well with Farmer Ken and Nishi so they wouldn't have minded the curious explorer sneaking around there house. In a close nit community like Golthwaite there was very rarely any crime so the village folk usually slept quite soundly in their beds. However if a member of the law enforcement community happened to be wandering by it could be looked upon as quite suspicious.

In Golthwaite, the law enforcement community consisted of P.C. Nicholas Fellans who very rarely got out of bed before mid-day, as due to the non existence of crime in the village, he had nothing to do. He would stay up late cycling around the village hoping to find a crime in order to justify his existence but was regularly left disappointed. He recently got quite excited when he found an abandoned crisp packet on the village green and launched a three week littering investigation into solving who had left it there. It turned out it had dropped out of his pocket not two minutes before he found it.

The would be sneak made his way up the stairs and crossed the landing placing an ear against every paper door that he passed, listening intently for any sign of life from behind. As he reached the final door, straining his fleshy auditory device, Jimmy suddenly pulled his head away quickly, a look of concern on his face at a strange sound from beyond.

That can't be right," he muttered, "I'm sure I just heard someone 'mooing'."

Tentatively he placed his head back in its previous position.

From behind the thin paper screen there came a muffled 'moo' as if someone was doing a cow impression. Most peculiar.

Then it happened again, but a little louder this time making Jimmy startle. Flossy's ears pricked up sharply.

"Mmoo, Mmoo." Could that be someone with a gag on shouting for help? Jimmy's mind was working overtime, trying to think what to do. (It had to do overtime because, due to time constraints, it couldn't think of everything in normal time.)

"Something's very wrong here," he whispered to Flossy. "Farmer Ken, I'm coming in, I'll help you!"

In a snap decision Jimmy took a few steps back, and then charged at the paper and bamboo door in an attempt to surprise the farmer's captors. All sorts of scenarios whirled through his mind with the pace of a documentary slide show – maybe armed raiders held them hostage, maybe they'd been bound and gagged by burglars in the night – whatever it was he was going to help. The brave fool.

Bursting through the paper and bamboo barrier he stopped in his tracks catching himself from tumbling over the bed, confusion returning to its rightful place upon Jimmy's face. There were no intruders to fight, no incarcerated occupants, just Farmer Ken in his blue and white striped pyjamas and Nishi in her similarly pink ones sat on the edge of their futon, both with slightly slanted eyes out of focus and staring into space. The couple's mouths were idly flapping like broken doors in the wind emitting the occasional cow call. The sight was quite disturbing. Flossy who had followed in closely behind Jimmy, surveyed the scene. She dropped on to her haunches and quickly evaluated the situation. The fur on her hackles raised, her teeth were bared slightly and she sniffed the air intently.

Almost in the man's face Jimmy pleaded, "Farmer Ken, Farmer Ken, what's wrong? What's going on?"

"Moo."

"Farmer Ken, please stop joking around." Turning to the farmer's wife. "Mrs Farmer Ken, what's wrong?"

"Moo."

"Please, you're scaring me now. Mrs Farmer Ken, please stop it."

"Moo."

"Moo."

In a frenzied state, Jimmy put his hands on the Japanese man's shoulder and gave him a gentle shake. The farmer's head wobbled like a balloon on stick and there was no cognitive response from him at all; his eyes were focused miles away.

Flossy jumped on the bed and barked at them, trying to get their attention or at least provoke a reaction. Nishi did not like having animals on her lovely silken sheets, so it was a cunning ploy.

Nothing.

"Moo."

Jimmy waved his hands in front of their faces.

Nothing.

He clapped and made loud raspberry noises.

Still nothing.

He tousled Farmer Ken's straight black hair.

Same response. Nothing.

"Think something's wrong with Farmer and Mrs Farmer Ken Flossy." Jimmy had a brilliant knack of stating the obvious. Flossy's face had the look of 'yeah, dah'.

"Why are they mooing and looking like they are trying to chew cud?" Ever the curious one, the young lad often had many questions and musings. Very rarely though was he ever able to come up with a suitable answer on his own.

Whilst in his moment of contemplation, Farmer Ken quite unexpectedly stood up, very stiffly like an automaton. He swivelled on the spot and started lumbering very slowly, one flat footed step at a time, towards the door. His hand reached out going through the motions of trying to slide open the screen door, even though Jimmy had smashed through it minutes earlier and most of it lay on the floor under the farmer's feet, and ventured across the landing towards the stairs. Nishi remained where she was, totally oblivious to all activity going on around her and quite content in her position.

Even though the farmer's back was turned, Jimmy heard something new coming from the blue striped pyjama clad zombie's lips.

"Mmiiilllk."

Jimmy quickly glanced at Nishi. Deciding she didn't look like she was going anywhere in a hurry, he curiously decided to follow the Japanese man on his trance like expedition.

"Did he just say milk?"

"Mmiiilllk."

"Why's he saying that? Is he sleep walking? It is milking time for the cows; that must be where he thinks he's going."

After what seemed an agonisingly long shuffle down stairs moving one laborious step at a time, an arduous traverse across the hall, another extensive shuffle across the living room then finally reaching the kitchen, the trancelike farmer ended his travels in front of the fridge door, only stopping himself by bumping straight into it face first.

In deliberate slow motion he took a step back, raised his arm like a car plant robot, opened the fridge door, reached inside and pulled out a bottle of full cream milk.

Only now did and expression of delight appear on his face.

"Moo….Mmiiilllk." And with that amazing piece of insight he lifted the bottle high, tipped his head back to face the ceiling, opened his mouth wide and proceeded to pour the contents all over his face.

The white stuff went everywhere except the place it should be going; what little did hit his mouth he gulped down with relish. A façade of inane pleasure crept on to his milk soaked face. The farmer's demeanour was one of euphoria as the chilled liquid drenched him from head to toe; totally soaking his jammies that now clung to rather well toned, well honed muscular frame of the little Japanese man.

'That's disgusting!' Jimmy gawped then screwed up his face at the lactose induced shower, 'although it is a lot better than drinking the rancid white stuff.'

You see Jimmy was unable to drink milk, chomp cheese, cram cream or yearn for yoghurt as he was lactose intolerant. The unbelievable thing is that neither he, nor his parents, actually knew this; he just thought that he didn't like dairy produce because of the taste and had historically refused to entertain eating or drinking it.

Milk made him ill, cheese gave him a chill, yoghurt made him vomit and cream made him scream. In fact now, as all this came back to him, he remembered and exclaimed aloud just to make sure, "I hate milk!"

He had never held this condition against the cows, though. It wasn't their fault that nature had chosen them to produce gallons of liquid evil every day which just happened to be enjoyed by millions of people every day on cereal, in coffee, in puddings, in milkshakes…the list is endless.

Gosh, isn't it a versatile ingredient as well as a good source of calcium that is vital for healthy bones and teeth – oops, this sounds like an advert for the Milk Marketing board. Sorry, but everyone should be aware of the health benefits of milk, even if it does leave you susceptible to Bovine mind control. We claim totally impartiality on these matters and have to give both sides of the argument you see therefore also don't forget the alternatives provided by goats and sheep.

It was enjoyed nowhere more than by the villagers of Golthwaite.

"Oh, Farmer Ken, you've made a right mess, and you'll catch a chill if you leave them wet jammies on." Surprisingly, Jimmy sometimes started to come into his own when a crisis emerged; he knew when harm was being done.

The warning fell on deaf ears though, as Farmer Ken was shivering yet insanely chuckling at the same time, his movements giving the impression he was being electrocuted, but doing nothing more than that. Jimmy grabbed a towel from a nearby radiator and started dabbing down the vibrating man.

What was going through this mental Oriental's head? This was very unusual behaviour – even for a man who exercised a number of ancient weird eastern mystical customs and rituals to discipline the mind.

Realising he was never going to get him dry whilst he was still wearing those soggy pyjamas, he stripped off the buttoned top, which Jimmy noticed was cotton (nowhere near as warm and comfy as his woollen jammies at home) and wrapped another towel he found lying in the nearby laundry basket around the farmer's shoulders. Farmer Ken offered no resistance at all, just stood on the spot merrily trembling; eye's staring off into the distance and mumbling the occasional moo accompanied by constant white drips coming from his extremities.

If all this behaviour wasn't weird enough, nothing could have prepared Jimmy for what he was about to see next. Right before his eyes Farmer Ken was developing black patches on his skin as though he were being plastered with a paintball gun. They were only faint but were appearing all over his torso; big blotchy patches splattered all over back and chest just like those of a....oh no...COW.

"Oh my gosh, you're becoming an Asian friesian!" Jimmy's jaw almost hit the floor after bouncing off his chest stomach and knees on the way down. "I knew nothing good could ever come from drinking milk, now look what's happened. We need to get you to the doctor. Now!"

Jimmy quickly finished rubbing down the flummoxed farmer and threw together the few bits of clothing he could find from the adjacent utility room. A flat cap, a pair of old worn corduroy slippers and a big brown raincoat. His top half looked ready for work, his bottom half looked ready for bed, considering he still had on his blue and white striped pyjama bottoms.

Having hastily prepared the farmer to face the outdoors in the face of a potential medical emergency, it was then that Jimmy realised he had another problem. The muddled agriculturalist, in his trance like state, didn't seem to want to be going anywhere in a hurry. In fact now he seemed to have stopped his previous oscillations and was standing very still again, his head now tilted back and slightly cocked to the side, mouth open, and eyes squinting whilst looking at the ceiling with a look of concentration on his face; almost as if he was straining to hear something. That emphatic grin was still spread across his face and now his eyes were partially hidden by the shock of sodden black hair that was plastered down his forehead adhered with dairy product.

"How do we move him Flossy? He doesn't seem to want to go anywhere." As if to emphasise the point, Jimmy gave him a little shove and Farmer Ken just wobbled backwards and forwards like a weeble that would wobble but it wouldn't fall down before again coming gently to a stop.

Flossy, who had all the time been sitting quietly in the background studying the events as they unfolded before her, stood up and patiently ambled over to the still open fridge, got up on her hind legs and stuck her long furry snout inside.

"This ain't the time to be thinking about your stomach girl."

Ignoring her owner's comments she triumphantly emerged with a large lump of cheddar cheese clasped firmly between her teeth.

"Urgh, put it away. Get it away from me Flossy; you know I hate the stuff."

The sheepdog continued to pay no attention to the young lad, once again shaking her head in response, and went and stood before Farmer Ken. Raising herself on her back legs and resting her front paws on the farmer's chest she waved the block of cheese in front of his face, letting him catch its heady odour. Ken's head snapped forward in instant recognition of the object before him, his clouded brown eyes strafing from side to side like a dizzy action man doll following Flossy's cheese waving action. A look of rapture appeared on his visage. Wherever Flossy moved with the cheese, Farmer Ken's attention followed, always intent upon the 'grande fromage'.

Jimmy stood in awe and amazement, even if he was a little disturbed by the presence of cheese. How had Flossy come up with that idea?

"What're you doing with that cheddar, Flossy, waving it around like that; you trying to torment me? And get off Farmer Ken, you'll mucky his coat with your dirty paws."

Once again turning a deaf ear to her master's selfish comments she lowered herself down from Farmer Ken and slowly started walking backwards towards the nearest door. Amazingly the Japanese man robotically lurched into action, arms stretched out in front of him in an attempt to claim the tempting cheddar.

"Cheeeeses," mumbled from the farmer's lips.

"Jesus indeed! Stop messing about Flossy or......Oh....I see," realisation dawned upon the young lad as rapidly as the rising of baking bread. Maybe Flossy had learned something from sheepdog school after all. "Good girl – of course, you're playing *chase the cheese!*"

Now I know what you're thinking, what in all the known universe is chase the cheese? Well, what you'll find in the country, is that some quaint country villages sometimes have their own quaint little country games and rituals often practised at celebratory events such as harvest festivals, May day and the old favourite high summer moon catching (these traditions do have to be kept up for the tourists you know). More often than not the origin of these traditions is lost in the annals of time and they quite often become diluted through the generations, each one putting their own stamp or mark or alteration upon it but they are still fun none the less.

Chase the cheese originated itself at such one of these festivals although no-one is sure which one as it has become so frequently played it has become a bit of a local sport. Funnily enough it tends to be played mostly on a Sunday afternoon when many of the village locals, after a ploughman's lunch and several pints of the landlord's traditional ale, start to take appreciation of the local cheese based produce (this is a dairy community of course – who else would relish cheese more than these fine folk? So quite often at closing time, when the landlord is wanting to clear out his pub of those troublesome locals who just don't want to leave, knowing their cravings for those late evening snacks will launch a wheel of fine cheddar or stilton (just a small one though, it would be a shame to waste it) out onto the village green declaring whoever can claim it, can keep it.

Well as you can imagine, this leads to much fun and frolics amongst the local residents in trying to obtain said cheese – the chase is then on! The results tend to be similar to a badly organised rugby match, quite often with similar tactics, until someone is fleet of foot enough to actually get away with the dairy prize

As it happens, Farmer Ken was rather good at this game for several reasons. Firstly he normally wasn't weighed down by several pints of heavy ale like the other tavern patrons with his preferred tipple being saki and secondly his legendary martial arts speed and skill made him a formidable adversary, giving him the edge of many of his burly opposition.

The popularity of this game has led to there being some rather vulgar individuals in the village as well as some local heroes, even amongst the womenfolk. It was surprising what the villagers would do for free cheese.

His competitive dairy craving instinct took over and the farmer was naturally drawn to the cheese.

Quite how Flossy had come up with this idea to get the stupefied farmer to move and make his way out of the house, Jimmy never thought to question, but it seemed to be working so he offered help and encouragement to his clever canine friend.

"Come on girl; let's get him to the doctor straight away. It's not that far from here though I'll bet he's not out of bed yet, so we're just gonna have to wake him – this is an emergency. Lead on lass."

Chapter 4

The village streets were still notably deserted as the early morning hours were quickly passing away. The gloopy silence shrouded Golthwaite until out of the absence something rather odd came into audible range.

Click, Click. Clack, Clack. Click, Click. Clack, Clack. Moo.

There, parading down the main street into the centre and making their way to the far side of the village, lined up with military precision, marching with the appearance of a melting chess board – the cows began to invade.

They lined the streets from wall to wall, a rolling Bovine barricade.

There was no-one to hinder their progress, no form of resistance – cleverly because the humans weren't actually aware they had anything to resist.

As the herd reached junctions and side streets, small groups splintered off beginning their own hike towards their designated coordinates within the village as allocated by Clover.

Like Daisy's elite group, each sub-command consisted of four cows led by a unit commander. You could identify these as the snotty ones with their nose in the air and a look of smug self importance.

Last in the line of the long parade were units two and seven and as they reached the furthest location away from the command centre they were right on the opposite side of the village to the Ken's farm.

Specifically chosen for this location as they were also led by two of the most experienced quad leaders, F.L.O.R.A. (First Leader of Resistance Administration) and C.L.E.V.E.R. (Command Leader Eliminator of Variable Enemy Resistance) – both quite apt names I think you'll agree and I promise, these names are all very circumstantial – you really couldn't make them up!

However, they had now been up since very early this morning and had been marching for about twenty minutes, a long time for a cow as they are normally used to lolling around in a field and don't normally wander very far, and as a result were getting a little tired and slightly bored.

Flora's tummies rumbled, "I'm getting hungry," she complained. "I missed breakfast this morning thanks to this marvellous invasion we're having. I think three of my four stomachs are rumbling like mad, I could murder some silage right now."

"I know what you mean," replied Clever. "But we can control the humans now. We shall have them bring us silage, or whatever else for that matter, whenever we want."

"Oh yeah, you're right. They will do whatever we want. Hah, this should be fun. In fact, what do you say we have a little fun with them right now?" Flora suggested mischievously.

Eyeing Flora warily, Clever replied, "Our orders are to secure the perimeter of the village, remember that. If Patch finds out you've been messing about, she'll have you on calf minding duty before you can say milking time."

"Aw come on, she'll never know. We're on the far side of the village. We can have a bit of a play as we mobilise the humans. Lighten up, it'll be fun. You're not sacred of *old blotchy leathers* are you?"

"No I am not, how dare you!" A slight curl of the lip. "Ok, but let's just be careful."

Both commanders mentally issued orders to the rest of their respective quads setting up a peripheral formation and gave the command to start bringing the people out of their homes by use of telepathy.

Concentration lined the wrinkled faces of the two quad lines as they faced towards neighbouring cottages, staring at them intently with silent determination.

Two of the team started shaking with the effort. These were the younger cows, around two or three years old, that had been placed within these commands to gain experience. This was the first time some of them had put their telepathy to use on humans and they weren't quite sure what to expect.

The feeling of rummaging around a human mind was alien to them and it wasn't pleasant. *They weren't even interested in eating grass.*

A young private was suddenly overwhelmed by a need to visit the toilet whilst wondering what they should wear at the same time and whether Tommy Monroe from number twenty two actually liked her or her best friend Kelly.

Strange you might think, but these were not her thoughts of course, but young Polly Templeton's from number twenty-one whose mind she was trying to invade.

"Concentrate ladies!" Flora encouraged. "Just remember your training. Let your mind flow with the milk, reach out and grab the pink pulpy minds of those dairy drinkers. Feel the link it has implanted in their tiny squishy brains and manipulate it to your will."

On hearing these words, the private relaxed. Perhaps a little too much too much as her bladder emptied on the pavement behind her as she was still in touch with the desperate toilet seeking Polly as the cerebral links were forming. Luckily the others didn't notice as they were all concentrating too.

Within the houses, any people that were awake and not already under the influence began to suddenly become confused and an unusual urge for dairy produce entered their thoughts. These people out on the village fringe may have just been out of range from the first assault from the cow shed, but were still groggy with the residual effects.

Being in various states of activity, they instantly stopped whatever they were doing. People fell over as they were trying to put on socks whilst standing on one foot, toothbrushes hit the floor, spoons fell into bowls, mugs of tea splashed everywhere.

Those who were still lucky enough to be in bed were none the wiser and would never figure out why they were having such beautiful dreams of cheese dipped in yoghurt.

Within moments freedom of thought fast became a memory and memories also became a, well, a memory as well. Until of course there were no more memories! Can you remember that?

It suddenly became apparent that all the inhabitants of those houses wanted to do was please those terrific, fabulous cows. In fact, they wanted to serve those very conveniently placed cows that were staring in at them through their windows.

Those beautiful, magnificent, glorious...

"Alright Private, enough of the cow glorification brainwashing," Clever shouted at one of her team. "I think they get the message."

"Sorry Ma'am."

"I think we have them all on this side of the street Flora, what about you guys?"

"Yes, we have them all," Clever replied, "time to start bringing them out."

"MMMMMmmmmmmoooooooo!" bellowed Flora.

Creepily, this was echoed from within the houses in rather a stifled manner.

"Good. Bring them out ladies."

Bangs, crashes, smashes and all other variations of collision based noises issued from within as under mental direction from the cows, who obviously couldn't see the interiors, the inhabitants within began to move around with the aim of exiting their houses. However, they were also trying to do this in the same zombified fashion as exhibited by Farmer Ken earlier, leading to bouts of clumsiness and scenes of extreme slapstickedness. There'd be a few bruises later.

Some of the victims had also diverted from their path as they felt the urgent need to visit refrigerators and have a little slurp of the white stuff as well. That was definitely a side effect that they would have to work on, but it was doing them no harm, the cows thought.

The first person emerged from their home and what a comical site it was.

It was Mrs Franklin at number sixteen who was quite apparently getting ready for one of her high society do's as she was wearing a rather splendid hat adorned with beautiful white ribbons and dainty little pink flowers. Unfortunately, apart from the hat, she wore little else but her enormous brilliant white grandma pants and hammock style bra. Both pieces of underwear were under enormous stress from the rolls of flabby skin trying to eject themselves from within their grasp. Not a pretty site.

It had to be said though, that she did know how to get those whites, dazzling white. As white as the milk beard she had dripping from her face.

"Oh this should be fun," Clever chuckled as she watched the stumpy hat adorned lady waddle towards her. "Hey, watch this."

She turned her full concentration on the figure before her who suddenly stopped in her doddery tracks, a flushed queer look on her face.

Amazingly, Mrs Franklin then started doing star jumps.

Up, wobble, down, wobble. The distressed look on her face showed that the actions taking place were in direct contradiction with what her mind would normally allow her body to do not to mention the straining underwear.

Clever and Flora were in hysterics, their big cow bellies rapidly inflating and deflating with each breathy snort.

"Ooohh, oh stop it. That was genius. I've got to better that." Gasped Flora.

The privates in the quads were looking bemusedly at their leaders, knowing that if they were to try anything like that then they would be seriously reprimanded, but they did allow themselves a little chuckle at the oscillating aerobic exposé.

More of the neighbourhood were now leaving their houses and were beginning to form into small groups along the pavements under the confidently growing instruction of the privates, eerily swaying on the spot in a uniform manner like trees in the breeze.

Occasionally, one of the humans would let out a small 'moo' but the majority of expressions wore blank indifference, with their surroundings seen through distant eyes, visible through masks of white where milk had been poured over their faces.

Flora spotted her target ambling along the road in drunken fashion and immediately began devising a devilish jest for this poor victim.

"You think your fatty's antics were funny, watch this!"

She had picked on skinny old Mr Winterton from number twenty-eight, a gentle old twiglet of a fellow who was often seen ambling around the village with his beech and gilt walking stick, tweeds and rather distinctive flat cap, (well it is Yorkshire, you know). He was the popular old man in the village, often found propping up the bar on Sunday lunchtime, telling stories about days of yore and how it was always better back then. He'd even been a bit of a cheese chaser in his younger years. Of course, this chap was fully dressed as, like all pensioners, he'd been up since four thirty in the morning and breakfasted before most sane people even entertained leaving the comfort of their beds even though, as most days, he had nowhere to go and nothing to do.

This particular morning Mr Winterton had been ritually stalking his letter box waiting for his morning paper to be delivered and was starting to get a bit grumpy as it was late. Little did he know that it would never arrive.

Now forced from his home, his zombie style walk was only exaggerated by his stiff limbed arthritic condition. Flora's next prank would be particularly cruel.

Mr Winterton halted on the spot, displaying the now common look of confusion of his wrinkled saggy face, and suddenly began to... body pop.

Undulating arms, swinging legs, limbs were moving all over the place before raising himself up more rigid to perform the 'robot', although the juddery action suggested an antiquated piece of machinery about to fall apart rather than a smooth fluid android.

"And now for my greatest trick," proclaimed Flora.

Mr Winterton was on the floor, gyrating, rotating, making some rather alarming snapping sounds, before achieving enough momentum to spin on to his back and ultimately raised to rotate on his head, his bald pate slipping on the silk lining of his flat cap it rested on and the walking stick held out as a glorious trophy to crown the move.

It was pretty fair to say he would wake up a little stiff and a bit bent out of shape later.

Flora and Clever were literally rolling around their backs now, not in a too dissimilar style to Mr Winterton, gasping for breath as guffaws erupted from their blotchy maws.

The privates, also caught up in the mood had a posse of other villagers line dancing in accompaniment to the free-styling before them; it was like a melted riverdance.

In the moment of mirth, mental concentration was beginning to slip and a few of the residents started to groggily become aware of their surroundings, eyes blinking into the bright daylight as recognition began to creep in that they weren't at home.

Noticing, Clever was quick to respond and professionalism once again took over.

"Privates, back to the task! That's enough high jinxes now. We have a job to do!" But quietly to Flora said,

"That was fun. We'll have to be careful though, a few of them nearly came round then."

"We'll be alright as long as the old patchy knickers doesn't find out, but I suppose we better get back to it, we might be running a bit behind now.

OK privates; let's move 'em out. Standard perimeter. Quick to it! Linked arms, half metre spacing"

All the beasts took big deep breaths to promote calmness and squeezed their brains really hard to start emitting the maximum amount of telepathic activity. Instantly, the humans suddenly went bolt upright and vacant again as they received their mental instruction and began wobbling into new positions.

"That's better, ladies," Flora encouraged her troop. "Spread them across roads and accesses, that's right. You two, blockade that junction. You, get that human back in line sharpish, good."

"Flora." Clever seemed to be studying something quite hard.

"Yes, Clever."

"Have you had any instructions from HQ over the last few hours?" She seemed quite concerned.

"Erm, now that I think of it, no. I can't hear them. Can you?"

"No, not a thing. All quiet. We seem to be cut off from the herd. I hope nothing's wrong."

"Ssh, not so loud, you'll worry the troops. We must be just out of mental range from command, that's all. I'm sure everything's fine, we'll just proceed as ordered. If anything changes I'm sure they'll send someone within range to deliver new instructions. But for now let's make sure we act as commanded and secure this outpost."

"I'm sure you're right. Old patchy must trust us enough to give us this assignment, let's make sure we get on with it; for the cause an' all that."

With a new sense of pride within themselves at realising they'd been chosen specially to hold this position on the frontier, they swore a little pledge that they wouldn't let their herd down. They were wily and experienced with enough ability between them to improvise at a moments notice should the situation require it.

That improvisation looked like it might be needed at any moment as coming down the main road leading into the village was a small white van, tearing up the tarmac towards them. Flora cast Clever a concerned look.

"COWS! To your stations!" Clever bellowed.

In seconds training kicked in and this was followed by a group of humans forming a chain and spreading themselves across the road then, quite eerily, standing very still.

Watching its rapid approach it looked like the van was in quite a hurry, yet strangely the driver looked rather vacant, obviously distracted by the large bacon and egg sandwich he'd obtained at his last delivery spot and eating it on the hop as he was running late.

As he took his next bite, a large dollop of runny golden egg yolk splurged forth from between the bun and slopped down the front of his neat white smock.

"Oh no, what the...., oh man!" His eyes looked down his front at the imminent yellow stain and lost contact with the road whilst he was negotiating a blind bend.

After assessing the ruin of his preciously sparkling overall, he managed a glimpse back through the windscreen and in sheer horror....

Screeeech.

The smell of burnt rubber invaded the air and the delivery man's face had suddenly gone the colour of his top. His breath rasped and his trembling hand no longer clutched the sarnie that was splattered all over the van floor.

"Aaah...." He was struggling to say much more than that as he began to realise how close he had come to mowing down the line of scantily dressed people before him.

Sucking in deep breaths he forced himself to calm down and assess the situation; *what's going on?* he thought to himself.

Leaning forward to peer through the windscreen at the line ahead of him he was mirrored with blank piercing stares, all very uncomfortable. Especially the site of some barely dressed old folks amongst them which were highly unpleasant to this young man.

Time slowed and for several moments nothing seemed to happen, they just stood.

And stared.

No-one moved.

Then…

Click-Clack. The cows came into view at either end of the line.

The driver jumped at their sudden appearance and it was now very apparent by the driver's body language that he was beginning to get very agitated.

"Oh no, this ain't right," he muttered to himself as he wound down the window. "Oi, what's going on? Get out o' the road you numpties. What're ya doin'? Some sort of protest? Well I ain't interested, just let me through, I got to get these papers to the newsagent and I'm already late."

No response.

His objections fell upon deaf ears.

He beeped the horn very long and very loud almost forcing his hand through the steering wheel.

They still didn't move.

Beep, Beep, Beee, Beeeeeep.

Suddenly, but very gradually the line broke in the middle and slowly started to part like a big human gate.

"About time," the driver muttered as he re-started his stalled engine and started putting the van into gear. He was just about to set of when," What the…?"

Standing in the gap between the once again static humans was a line of six cows in addition to the two at the ends, all slowly advancing towards him very ominously. Their steps in perfect time, and their legs in unerring synchronicity portraying a vision of intent.

Click, Click. Clack, Clack. Click, Click. Clack, Clack.

The advance was slow, steady deliberate.

The driver's eyes widened and his heart began to race. Never had he seen anything like this before.

As their intention became clear panic set in. Hands and feet all over the place, the driver fumbled with the gear stick and foot pedals as well as beginning to have a large craving for something milky or cheesy.

Closer and closer.

The driver began to feel himself become increasingly numb, his thoughts turning to yoghurt and cream.

Sweaty hands and feet slipping, the van stalled again, eventually followed by the continuous sounding of the van's horn as the driver's head hit the steering wheel falling into dreams of velvety white creamy milk.

The cows looked satisfied with themselves as they issued cerebral instructions to the other surrounding humans, two of whom in turn removed the driver from his vehicle and dragged him into their ranks.

Some time later the local bus arrived, and there before it in the road was a white van and beyond that a human gate blocking the way.

There, in the middle of the line was a man in white, a vacant expression on his face and a big yellow splotch of egg down the front of his white tunic linking arms with Mrs Franklin and Mr Winterton on either side.

Unseen, in the background, a small group of cows watched in menacing glee as the passengers got out to investigate what was going on.

More posts for the human fence.

Chapter 5

It was quite a comical sight to behold.

There they were, a shaggy black and white sheepdog, walking backwards, waving a cheddar around in front of a robotic farmer in his overcoat and slippers walking zombie fashion with his arms stretched out before him intent upon claiming the cheesy reward in the canine's jaw whilst all the time being excitedly championed and encouraged by a young lad dressed in his woollies and wellies down a deserted village lane at five o'clock in the morning.

But, unknown to this unlikely trio, they were being followed by four funny friesians, who quite amusingly, were plodding behind them at a respectable distance in a comical attempt to be covert, whilst hiding behind conveniently placed cars and bushes. Their eyes and attention were so intent on the weird trio however, that they weren't concentrating on their cover enough as they could have easily been spotted from a plane at twenty thousand feet. Luckily though, the three targets in question were so intent upon their own task it played in the cows favour.

A visitor that may have arrived in the village at that very moment and cast eyes upon this very scene would have thought the place to be barking mad, packed up their belongings, jumped back in their car and left immediately.

"Target spotted. Closing in Ma'am," Buttercup reported. "What are our orders? Are we to intercept the suspect?" She was always eager to please, but often seen as a bit of a creep by her counterparts.

"Patience, patience, we must first determine what this shabby wool encrusted little human is up to. I still can't sense any thoughts coming from him, can anyone else?" Head shakes all round. "It appears he's somehow found a way to override the telepathy over our silly little farmer, our main asset on the farm; Patch is not going to be pleased with this. Worse still he's using one of our own dairy products to do it and that stinks. It's as though he's mocking us."

"You're right," agreed Hyacinth. "I can't lock on to the farmer's mind at all anymore. The intense cheesy pull is diverting his mind into not accepting telepathic instruction. He's still under the influence but not directly receptive."

Through half squinted eyes Daisy studied the teenager. "This small one is cleverer than we thought."

The small clever on was getting a bit excited.

"Ha Ha, chase the cheese, chase the cheese!" Jimmy was jumping up and down and running round and round in a hysterical manner like a puppy waiting for its owner to throw a ball. 'Chase the cheese' always seemed to bring out the 'inner maniac' within everyone.

"You go Flossy, he'll never catch you." Which was in fact the whole point or they would never get the farmer anywhere in a hurry despite the fact he was moving like an animated corpse.

"We're nearly at the doc's now, keep going."

The streets and lanes were still empty as they reached the doctor's house which was located on the corner of the village green, actually quite close to Jimmy's house so he knew him quite well. It commanded a grand view across the whole common area and duck pond; a most desirable property.

On a whim, Jimmy suddenly turned round and scanned across the green behind him, scrutinising the village in view through narrowed eyes; there was a tingling sensation down the back of his neck. He couldn't explain it but he had a sudden feeling they were being watched – but from where?

Were the long shadows from the low early morning sun playing tricks on his eyes? For starters, that nearby lamppost looked slightly thicker than a normal one and he didn't remember any of them ever being painted with black and white patches.

Why did that wooden bench have eight legs, four of them with cloven hooves – was it some kind of new design he never seen before?

The cow on the billboard poster on the side of the bus shelter advertising the Golthwaite dairy looked awfully lifelike – it was almost three dimensional; and he could swear it just blinked.

But strangest of all there, just stood at the end of the street staring straight at him was a cow.

It must have followed me from the farm, Jimmy thought, *thinking it was going for milking.*

Farmer Ken would not be happy that one of his prized dairy cows had got loose, lucky there was no traffic about or the scene could have been one chaotic mess.

It appeared Dandelion still hadn't quite got the hang of covert operations and was performing rather poorly.

Daisy who was mimicking a lamppost desperately started barking orders, "I said stay out of sight you moron. What are you doing? You're stood in open view, you idiot?"

Dandelion was hurt. "I'm not in open view Ma'am, I blending in with this zebra crossing, there should be no way he can see me." It was true she was standing smack bang in the middle of the black and white pedestrian crossing in the middle of the road and she was quite pleased with herself for thinking of it.

"You fool, that would only work if he was viewing you from above. Does he look like he's flying? Has he suddenly sprouted wings? Is he currently hovering above you looking down upon you asking '*oh, I wonder where that cow went, it was there a moment ago but now all I'm up here I can see is this zebra crossing*'?" Cow sarcasm never ceases to amaze. "No, he's looking directly at you, which means only one thing – he can see you, you great Sunday lunch. Get out of there now and when we get back to headquarters you and I are going to have another strongly worded briefing session about the importance of camouflage."

"Oh no!" Dandelion paled, or rather her black patches went slightly greyer, as she realised the position she had got herself in. Embarrassing would be an understatement.

Obviously Jimmy had no comprehension of the scene before him or the interchange that had just taken place between the commander and squad member but what followed did amuse the young lad.

He watched in fascination at what could only be described as a tip-toeing cow retreating backwards looking almost sheepish, not really a good term for describing a cow and they would have found it an insult but you'll get the idea, with its head drooped down between its forelegs. Strangely the cow never took her eyes from the boy which only added to Jimmy's mirth as the daft friesian's backside kept bumping into everything from cars to lampposts.

Jimmy chortled out loud when one of the beast back legs got tangled up with its udders and it nearly fell flat on its rump.

By the time the silly moo had rounded the last bend and was finally out of site, after what felt like long agonizing moments to all the Bovines present, with several bins knocked over and at least two car alarms blurting out, Daisy finally breathed out, releasing the mounting tension that had grown with very impact Dandelion had made. It was a good job that none of the residents could hear such a commotion, she thought or there would have been an ungainly scene.

"I think it is best ladies that we don't report this to Patch, what do you say?" Daisy voiced warily.

"Aye." Hyacinth and Buttercup keenly replied in unison.

However, Jimmy was in hysterics.

The thought never crossed his mind that it should be unusual to find a cow walking backwards down a village lane. It was more that he'd just never seen a cow walking backwards at all, especially one impersonating a pinball, ricocheting around the obstacles in the street like that, its eyes screwing up and face cringing with each impact. It never occurred to him that no-one was responding to the car alarms either. It had even slipped his mind the trouble caused should the cow be found to have got loose from the farm. His mind was so easily distracted. He carried on laughing.

A short time later, after getting his breath back and rubbing his now aching tummy to release the tension, Jimmy took a few deep calming breaths and forced himself to re-focus on the task at hand. The ever vigilant Flossy had now cleverly guided the lurching farmer to the gates of the doctor's house, although Jimmy never once thought to himself *how does she know the way* as he wasn't leading them.

The doctor's house and garden were always pristinely presented and the physician always prided it as the gem of the green. It was a slightly larger building than was found in the rest of the village as it housed his surgery as well as his home and sat on the corner of the road that circled the village common and pond. Of course, he had to portray the image that he was an upstanding pillar of the community, you know.

Jimmy walked up to the jet black gloss garden gate that sat between two perfectly symmetrical, squared off, equally high privet hedges flanking it on either side.

On the gate there was a brass plaque reading 'Dr. Healsnaught – General Practitioner'. The doctor was very proud of that plaque and was often seen polishing it on Sundays.

Jimmy opened the gate and entered the long, formal garden that had a beautiful granite stone sett cobbled path leading up to the front door, as straight as a Roman road. This was bordered on both sides by perfectly aligned flower beds full of amazing coloured plants of all varieties with velvet mown lawns beyond them. Dr Healsnaught was very proud of his garden, he loved the formal drama of the approach to the house as he thought it brought him a sense of grandeur but it was believed most of the success was down to his wife who was very green fingered.

By now Flossy had managed to guide Farmer Ken into the garden but the Japanese man had suddenly veered off course and was now wading his way through a patch of pink begonias.

"Flossy, quick get him under control quickly, or the doctor will have us for trampling his plants!"

Jimmy shot up the path to the front door as Flossy managed to direct the farmer onto the lawn and now had him going round and round in circles in an attempt to distract him until Jimmy could get the doctor to open up and let them in.

The young lad banged the big shiny chrome door knocker that he could see his reflection in and was located perfectly central in the panelled gloss black front door, which then sat symmetrically in the centre of the grand grey stone house. He continued to create a racket until, at last, a key could finally be heard turning in the lock, accompanied by a deep muffled grumbling voice, and a tiny crack began to appear as the door opened slightly to be held by a rattling chain. A questioning bleary eye appeared in the niche.

"Who is it at this un-godly hour in the morning? Honest folk are trying to get their beauty sleep you know. We doctors aren't like you farmers, we work normal civilised hours," the shiny black door proclaimed.

"Dr Healsnaught, it's Jimmy Tatley, we have an emergency and need your help. There's something seriously wrong with Farmer Ken."

"Emergency you say, it better be or I may create an emergency situation of my own with you boy."

The crack disappeared as the door closed.

Clunk, clank, click, rattle, whir, creak. Dr Healsnaught did seem to have an over emphasis on security, which was quite strange for a low crime community although sometimes the physician did attract a lot of weirdoes to his house of which many were farm related with today being no exception, and he did like his privacy; he was so stuffy sometimes.

The opening process seemed to be taking an eternity.

Jimmy looked round to see Farmer Ken was now beginning to wear a donut shape on the lawn where Flossy was leading him round and round in an attempt to keep him occupied and starting to look dizzy. The doctor had every right to be locked up tight, Jimmy acknowledged.

The door swung open and a stout, middle aged man stood in front of Jimmy wearing nothing but a pair of green paisley boxer shorts, over which an ample belly with a cavernous belly button was hanging, and a woollen nightcap; a lovely deep sage green one with a daffodil yellow pom-pom hanging from the end swinging around his ear (this caught Jimmy's attention straight away and helped distract the attention away from the lardy mound before him).

The doctor was yawning, exposing the fillings at the back of his mouth, rubbing the sleep out of his bloodshot eyes with one hand whilst simultaneously scratching his gratuitous rear end with the other. It was clear that the doctor was not used to being awake at this time of the morning in the company of visitors.

"Erm, nice cap doctor." Jimmy chuckled.

The doctor looked up, tilting his head back, to see what the boy was talking about making the pom-pom dance around his shoulders.

"What? Oh. Well, er, it was cold last night lad, got to keep your head warm, you know."

Jimmy marvelled at this statement as it would have taken a bed sheet the size of a ships sail to cover this fellow up and keep him warm due to his considerable midriff, never mid his head.

Although Dr Healsnaught was a respected physician within the village and also within his profession, he was never able to follow his own health advice. More of a 'do as I say, not as I do' man. He smoked like a chimney, drank like a fish, with a weakness for a fine brandy, and held the village record for pie eating. He was also the chase the cheese record holder with over a hundred wins under his belt; you would never have known looking at him. Therefore he wasn't the figure of health and fitness that he preached that his patients ought to be.

The doctor had a particular penchant for cheese. Whether it was cheese and biscuits, cream cheese, cheese on toast, cheese cake (hence the record) – he was an incredibly cheesy man. At this present moment he was carrying the slight odour of stilton.

"Now what seems to be the problem young Jimmy, it is incredibly early you know?" His eyes drifted towards the cheese chasing farmer creating crop circles in his garden before widening and saying "Oh, I see."

"Sorry for waking you up so early, but Farmer Ken's been acting very strangely and so has Mrs Farmer Ken. He keeps mooing like a cow and then poured milk all over himself. He keeps chasing this cheese that Flossy has, even doing it whilst sleepwalking. We had to bring him here with cheddar."

"Umm, how peculiar, that's very strange behaviour indeed, better get him inside before that ring in my lawn becomes a trench." Motioning with a waving hand, he directed them inside and as he was doing so his eyes caught sight of something rather odd. "I don't remember having any black and white coloured bushes," he mumbled questioningly.

Catching what he said, Jimmy turned in the direction the doctor was looking but saw nothing but the prickly privet hedges. "What do you mean, doctor?"

"Maybe it's me; I don't think I've quite woken up yet." He rubbed his eyes removing the last remnants of sleep. "Aah, well come on, in you come you er...three."

"Lead him in Flossy, good girl."

Through further cheese enticement they herded the farmer through into the doctor's house much to the amazement and amusement of Dr Healsnaught.

With a little bit of assistance they managed to get the zombie cheese chaser into the surgery and sat him on a worn brown leather couch.

Dr Healsnaught's surgery made Jimmy feel like he'd stepped back in time. The dark oak wooden panelled walls, the old cherry wood bureau that the doctor used as his desk, the black and white marble tiled floor were all very nostalgic.

An antiseptic smell of salves and unguents hung in the air. Jars and bottles of unusual shapes lined the shelves around the room. An air of mystery was added by the dim light that came from the replica oil lamps on the wall and the colourful stained glass lantern in the roof.

The doctor still hadn't bothered to cover himself up and wobbled his way over to examine the farmer bringing with him the trusty tools of his trade that he'd pulled from his medical bag near the desk.

"Right, let's have a look at him. Mmmm…dilated pupils, delayed reaction to stimuli, increase in temperature and….ooh, was that you? Ergh, that smells terrible."

"It wasn't me," said Jimmy defensively.

A rumbling trumpet issued forth from Farmer Ken's behind.

"Blimey, better check that out, it smells a bit rancid." The physician put his stethoscope to the farmer's tummy, farmer Ken never even jumped at its cold touch. "Goodness, he's bubbling like a volcanic mud pit in there, doesn't sound good at all."

His comment was greeted with another methane fanfare, followed by another, and another. He was becoming quite regular. Before long the surgery was beginning to smell like an old folk's home after a chilli supper.

The doctor's face turned an off shade of crimson and sweat began to drip from his wrinkly brown. The room was beginning to get warmer and the air was becoming a bit thick and pungent.

"Phew, it appears he's warming things up a bit in here, isn't he!" Even the doctor's humungous belly was starting to glisten with tiny drops of perspiration. "Just take this off I think." He removed his woolly nightcap exposing his shiny bald pate. "Aah, that's better, now…then….let's…..er…err…moo?"

"Sorry doctor, let's what now?" Jimmy queried.

"I mean, ahem, I think I…er…better…erm….Moo. Mooo." An anxious look came from Dr Healsnaught as he struggled to form any coherent words.

"My gosh Flossy, did you hear that. Doc, are you all right?"

The doctor's expression was slowly changing to mimic that of the farmer. It advertised brain for rent – thoughts apply within.

Jimmy waved his hand in front of the doctor's big red podgy face and got no response from him at all. His blubbery body had gone limp and his big round shoulders now sagged. Cow calls continued to issue from his mouth.

Strangely, the young lad's normally carefree attitude felt itself being shoved over by something he wasn't accustomed to feeling and that was worry. Jimmy was often used to feelings of confusion, most of the time even that didn't register with him it was that so common, but this time he instinctively felt there would be consequences if he didn't act upon this strange emotion this time.

He started to put the pieces together in his mind; an action similar to a hundred piece jigsaw being assembled by a toddler but he began to rationalize eventually.

Firstly, people were starting to moo - like cows.

Secondly, the farmer was obsessed with dairy produce – from a cow.

Thirdly and unusually, objects in the street were starting to look – like cows.

There were cows roaming free in the farmer's back yard that also looked like – well, like cows really.

Synapses fired, links formed and a vague connection began to form in the deep undiscovered chasms of Jimmy's brain, the strain was visibly showing on his features and his ears were turning bright red with the effort, but try as he might, he just couldn't identify the missing link.

As Jimmy examined the stricken pair before him he thought, the doctor was ok until....he took his woolly nightcap off and....

"That's it! Everyone's catching cow disease through their heads," he beamed with delight at his terrible conclusion. "Therefore they are rejecting wool. It's coming from all those cows that are wandering about. When he took his hat off he wanted to be a cow. Think I'll have that cap – I don't want to be a cow!"

Flossy fell over in disbelief at what she was hearing.

Jimmy popped the ridiculous green and yellow headwear on his noggin. Ah, cosy, he loved wool. It suddenly started to give him a slight buzzy tingly feeling like hundreds of flies tap dancing on his scalp. Grey cells that hadn't been used since they were first formed at birth began to vibrate and whir into action. Synapses exploded, well more likely fizzled a bit. Jimmy thought it was just warming his head up a bit.

Then something happened that had never occurred before in Jimmy's short life so far, he had a Eureka! moment.

"On second thoughts Flossy, I think the cows are up something. That's what that little robin was trying to warn us about. They have cleverly devised a way to control the minds people using dairy produce and are going to enslave the human race. But their immediate priority is to establish control in this village and we have to stop them."

After just picking herself up, Flossy's jaw plummeted to the ground on hearing her master's revelations, not because of what she was hearing, of course she'd worked it out long ago but because she was actually surprised he had worked it out for himself.

Or had he?

She suspected unseen help from somewhere and had suspicions as to who it would be but she couldn't let on to her owner. The woollen cap had certainly helped in some way and her nose was tingling at the introduction of some unknown force.

On the other hand, you never know, there may actually be hope for the young lad yet.

Jimmy actually looked surprised with himself. He didn't know he had it in him. A smug grin formed as he vowed never to forget this day. His parents would be so proud.

"So what do we do Flossy, how can us two stop a herd of cows?" Well he couldn't continue with the rich vain of form of cerebral aptitude he had newly discovered just yet, one step at a time. "They're bigger than us, smarter than us..." It seems they weren't *dumb* anymore now he knew the truth. Flossy's face screamed *speak for yourself* "... and there're more of them. What can we do?"

Flossy gravely considered this question momentarily before getting up onto her feet and moving to pick up the piece of cheese that she'd been enticing Farmer Ken with earlier. She then placed herself in front of Jimmy and sat down looking directly into his eyes making sure she had his full attention.

Rapidly she chomped down on the cheddar spraying pieces in all directions, then raised her head and looked up the young lad hopefully, pleased with her dramatic gesture tongue lolling out to one side.

"Of course, that's it, well done girl. We have to squash all the cheeses."

Flossy deflated.

"Wait a minute, squash all the cheeses? What would we accomplish with that? What you getting at Flossy?"

The sheepdog puzzled for a moment her eyes scanning the room for something that might aid her. After a few seconds she seemed to agree something in her mind with a slight nod of the head and began to toddle off through the surgery door into the corridor beyond.

Intrigued, Jimmy obediently followed. Before he passed through the door Flossy had just entered, he quickly glanced around to observe the bizarre scene of both the doctor and the farmer on their hands and knees with their heads bobbing up and down towards the floor as the grazed on the cheese remnants the dog had just left behind, merrily mooing as they did so. He looked at them with disgust.

"How can anyone eat that stuff – it's horrible?" he mused as he held back the gagging reaction at the back of his throat. He left the room desperately trying to remove the weird image from his mind.

The lad caught up with his dog in Dr Healsnaught's kitchen although it felt more like a hospital operating theatre. There was a surgical cleanliness in the air that clung to the stark glossy white cupboards and stainless steel counter tops. Everything was placed with accuracy and precision. Jimmy wondered if the physician actually carried out operations in here instead of cooking.

Luckily the curtains had not been pulled back as Jimmy was sure he would have been dazzled by any reflections from any sunlight entering the room.

Flossy began nosing at the shiny metal American style fridge.

"Not again, you've been fed girl. You can't be hungry yet."

She began to paw at the door creating paw marks on the glossy front.

Urgently Jimmy said, "Stop that. Ok, you win. Let's see what you're getting at."

He opened the door and examined the contents within.

There were countless types of exquisite cheese (as you would expect from a connoisseur such as the doctor), a big block of golden butter, a large bottle of milk and a few fruit and vegetables (obviously an influence from the doctor's wife who was strangely absent, though Jimmy hadn't noticed). That was it, Jimmy's nose screwed up.

Also surveying the products before her, Flossy's nose immediately pointed at the bottle of milk (ironically from Farmer Ken's farm) so Jimmy nervously pulled it out of the fridge and placed it on the white lacquered table nearby.

The determined canine jumped up and then proceeded to knock it over, the white liquid spilling over the edge and dripping to the floor into a big pool. Once again she turned her gaze towards her owner with a look of expectation and then started stamping on and growling at the puddle that was forming beneath the table.

"We have to get rid of the milk?"

Flossy's eyes lit up a slight curl of a smile appearing around her snout, her tongue lolling in enthusiasm.

"We have to get rid of the milk! But not just that - all dairy products! Clever girl." This appealed greatly to Jimmy due to his obvious distaste for the stuff. "Hang on….. all of it?" He scratched the back of his head in apprehension at the enormity of such a task.

He could swear Flossy was nodding.

"That's a huge thing to do lass; those cows produce gallons of the stuff daily. It would be easier to stop them making it and then that would be some achievement."

The would be dairy saboteur turned his mind towards the task, looking for some inspiration as to how to complete this near impossible dilemma the grey matter was faced with, but on the road it was struggling to come to terms with what it was up against his mind turned back – in a complete u-turn. Random thoughts began to escape though, quite how we'll never know, but all ideas have got to come from somewhere even if they from the most improbable source.

"To stop the cows from being milked," Jimmy thought aloud, "we have to stop them from getting to the milking shed. But there are so many of them, so we can't do that. We're greatly outnumbered."

Flossy already seemed to have a solution to the problem. She padded over to Jimmy and started nosing in his pocket trying to establish the contents inside. Jimmy delved his hand in deep and turned out the knick-knacks within to see what she might be after.

One stick of chewing gum, he was saving that for later. One ten pence piece, just in case he needed to phone his mum. One pebble, well it was a lovely reddy brown colour and very glossy and smooth – why not? Then last but not least, his shiny metal sheep herding whistle. It appeared this was the object that the curious canine was looking for.

"Herd them Flossy? Could we do that? How?"

Flossy's looked up at her master frustrated at her inability to make him understand. She looked as if she was up to the challenge herself. It would certainly be more exciting than herding those dreary sheep who followed each other around in a flock, a cotton wool raft afloat on a sea of green grass. However, Flossy knew she couldn't do this alone and they would require help. Her eyes drifted back to the whistle in the young lad's hand. Help would come if required.

Outside the surgery and slightly down the lane, Daisy's elite unit had reformed after Dandelion's earlier blunder and were now conferring in an old abandoned outhouse they had found at the end of someone's garden.

Dandelion had received a severe dressing down and was looking a little chagrined but this was brushed aside by the others as they planned their next move. There was work to do.

It was a bit cramped as you can imagine, trying to fit four cows into a small stone building no bigger than a large shed. If they had been squeezed in any tighter they were in danger of coming out the other side as mince. However, they were trying to stay out of sight from this mysterious young boy who seemed to be walking around with a mind of his own – something that would not be tolerated. One close call today was already enough.

Daisy was summing up to her team, "We need to apprehend and detain this young human male as per our orders. He seems to have conjured a way to obstruct our mind control, but not only that he also seems to be able to manipulate other humans as well that are already under our telepathic influence. We all saw how he was leading the farmer with the cheese.

That canine companion of his also seems to be aiding him in some way, I feel that she is some sort of counter agent but we don't have the time or resources to deal with her as well. We'll just report that back to the Commander.

Also I have observed he is wearing some sort of protective armour that looks like wool. I haven't seen armour like that since back in the days of the Moor Wars with those troublesome Ovies Aries (that's sheep to you and me but sometimes cows like to sound a bit clever by using fancy Latin terms, which in itself is just showing off as why would they bother to learn human Latin in the first place?), "but surely they wouldn't try to interfere. Not again. How would they know our plans?"

"So what are we to do now Ma'am?" Hyacinth asked whilst trying to turn her head around to face the commander, but was hampered in her progress by the gratuitous size of Buttercup's rump that was in her face – it was small outhouse.

"I suggest the 'distract and pincer' movement. Hyacinth you're assigned decoy as he's already seen you wandering around, Buttercup you're to the rear,

Dandelion you're the 'surprise'. I'll move in for the intercept and capture."

"Oh yes, the good old BBS..." Buttercup's eyes slid into the past reminiscing on previous manoeuvres.

Bewilder, bungle and squash; an old Bovine military tactic for catching human prisoners. Essentially it comprises of one cow laying down feigning illness or injury. This then draws the unwitting human towards them, drawn in by their heart-warming compassion to help a beast in distress as let's be fair; we softy animal lovers can't help ourselves can we. Two other cows will then sneak up behind the human thus distracted by the decoy. One will lay directly behind the victim and the other stands ready to pounce and detain. The fourth remaining cow will then endeavour to take the human by surprise of which there are also many tactics employed, each cow having their own particular favourite. But the most acceptable practice is 'jumping' (if you can imagine a cow jumping) out from behind some form of concealment. Once 'surprised' the human is triggered into stumbling backwards falling over the cow strategically placed behind them. Once sprawled upon the ground the detaining cow will then sit upon them, rendering the target helpless until they have either passed out from lack of oxygen or just merely from the smell. As you can probably imagine, this all looks very comical. Straight from the 'how to perform slapstick comedy' manual of practical jokes. It is rumoured that it is the cows that formed the origin of the popular playground prank but of course that could never be proved as no-one knows its exact history.

The black and white pranksters 'sprang' – or gently moseyed – into position biding their time and awaiting their prey.

Things are still being monitored...

"Report!"

"Cows have been spotted on village perimeters."

"Their tactics don't appear to have changed much over the years."

"At least we know what we are dealing with now."

"The emissary is yet unharmed and we believe is formulating plans with the guardian."

"Some assistance has been provided."

"With any luck he will act soon and further aid won't be required."

"We'll keep our hooves crossed."

"We can't leave this up to luck! We must remain vigilant and prepared at all time and defeat them with a well ordered and structured resistance."

"Of course, it was a flippant remark. Apologies."

"Not necessary, just do your job and we'll be fine."

"Oooh, look a four leaf clover, I'm having that!"

Chapter 6

Jimmy and Flossy set off; a look of grim determination chiselled on the young lads face, an even grimmer one on the canine's. His mind was working with a focus and intensity he'd never felt before.

Leaving the doctor's house, Jimmy shut the glossy black gate behind them, when suddenly Flossy's ears pricked up, her body halted rigid in alertness and she began to emit a low cautionary growl as she instinctively scanned the vicinity.

"What's up girl?" Jimmy asked as his eyes followed the sweeping line of her gaze which finally settled on a stricken cow laid across the middle of the road a short distance away.

"Isn't that the daft cow that was walking backwards earlier on?" Jimmy's excellent ability with animals allowed him to identify individuals of a species as easily as humans recognise one another after a first meeting. He chuckled again as he remembered this one's earlier exploits. "I bet it's gone and got itself knocked over. Why isn't anyone helping it? That's disgraceful. Better go and check if it's alright."

It still hadn't occurred to him that there were still was still no-one around or even a faint murmur of traffic in the background.

Flossy immediately jumped in front of him with a look that portrayed *oh no you don't*. Her interference was in vain though as Jimmy's deep humanitarian and empathic nature towards animals had already kicked in at the sight of an animal in distress – he couldn't override the overwhelming urge to help.

"It's ok Flossy; it can't harm me, not if it's injured anyway. I just want to make sure it's not suffering that's all. Even in war it's not fair to let an enemy suffer needlessly." Jimmy was a very compassionate lad with the heart the size of a textile mill.

With this reasoning Flossy relented slightly and conceded the point, but her animal instinct, that extra sixth sense that all animals seem to possess, still suggested something was amiss here. She knew cows were not to be trusted, even seemingly helpless ones.

Flossy suspected a deception but didn't know how she could communicate this to her aid rendering master. So the loyal canine stood her ground though whilst Jimmy casually wandered over to the suspiciously prone Bovine.

As the dog watched, the outrageous spectacle that occurred next appeared to happen in slow motion. This isn't too far from the truth where cows are concerned as they are hardly known for their speed or rapidity - as you've already found out.

Two cunning cows crept out from behind a nearby bush and rather awkwardly tip-hoofed (they have no toes) behind Jimmy who was down on his haunches examining and tending to the stricken beast. He'd adopted a rather studious look as he studied in great detail the cow's demeanour, before eventually nodding his head as he concluded to himself that, yes; she was laid down in the road.

Buttercup, in stealth mode, slowly but surely laid down behind Jimmy and Daisy stood close by poised in anticipation.

Amazingly, due to the overwhelming need to care for the injured animal on the floor and the concentration he was greatly exuding, the young lad never even noticed the appearance of two large black and white beasties in his vicinity.

This was much to the dismay of Flossy who was becoming fearful upon the Bovine appearance. Watching the whole spectacle in sheer disbelief at what was happening, she hoped that her misled master would at least come to his senses, look around and see what was occurring.

No such luck.

The smart mutt sensing the danger but also realising there was nothing she could do about it, sank on to her belly she slinked away, trying to blend in to her surroundings in an attempt to become unnoticed. She seemed to be succeeding as they certainly hadn't caught sight of her yet and only seemed to be interested in the young boy they were trying to ensnare.

Then with the grace, elegance and dynamasism of an inebriated snail Dandelion exploded (walked at a slow human pace) out from behind a nearby bus shelter and in front of Jimmy letting loose with an almighty "MOO"; it was really quite a display. Very impressive.

Jimmy slowly and casually raised his head, blinked twice, eyed the cow in annoyance before addressing this would be jack-in-the-box and calmly said "Keep it down, will you; there's an injured cow here. Don't worry though I think your friend's ok, nothing serious."

Dandelion froze.

What should she do next? This young human boy was amazing, as again, he was totally unfazed by her presence; he seemed to have outwitted another one of their ploys.

Her companions were also standing there gawking in disbelief. This method was tried and tested, what went wrong?

There was only one thing for it – time for plan B.

Lowering her head, Dandelion slowly lolled her way directly towards Jimmy, who at this point had stood up to stretch his weary legs, and…..she walked straight into him.

Now Jimmy was surprised.

He reeled over backwards, stumbled over Buttercup laid behind him (who amazingly he still hadn't noticed) and landed flat on his back with a bruising thump.

"Ow! What? Where did you come from? AAaagh!"

A deep shadow suddenly fell across him blotting out the sky above; the air became very earthy, thick and smelly. Jimmy suddenly began finding it hard to breathe.

A large black and white blur moved into view, ominously hovering above him as he looked upwards still laid out in his helpless position before descending slowly and deliberately towards him.

Becoming light headed, dread took over as he grasped the situation he was in. Panic arose which only made the breathing harder. The weight on his chest was growing

Three cows moved in to his restricted peripheral vision, long snouts with snotty pink noses leered down at the stricken boy from either side of the giant tail swishing cow rump that was directly in his face, their eyes shimmering with amusement.

Only at this point did he realise he had been duped.

He began to flail around looking for any source of help.

He tried to call but he couldn't catch a breath, his vision was beginning to fade.

He was trapped; he could only just wiggle his toes and fingers.

Where was Flossy?

Straining now to even move his head, his vision blurring through watery eyes, he just about spotted her at a distance from between the legs of the surrounding cows.

She was so far away.

"Flossy...Where…help….girl….."

He watched as, slinking away on her belly, she turned her back away from them and fled down the street.

She had deserted him.

Left him.

Alone.

When he needed her most.

But wasn't she was always loyal?

As his eyes finally closed he began to feel very foolish, helpless, alone and a little scared.

Then all went black.

Don't Panic!

"We believe the emissary has been caught!"

"Caught? How?"

"The Bovines have surmised that the boy is a danger to them but they don't understand why. We believe they have captured him for study to determine if this flaw in their plan would be a problem for them."

"We don't think they will harm him for now as they are still curious, but they may still dispose of him once they have fathomed out his strength and the weakness in their plan."

"Let's pray that doesn't happen soon."

"What about the guardian?"

"She is still free. We expect her to report shortly with a possible plan of rescue and receive further instructions on this situation."

"That's good, we will need her input."

"Start mustering the brigade, we must prepare for immediate mobilisation should our aid be required."

"We are now on high alert everyone – don't let me down!"

"Typical, I haven't had my breakfast yet!"

Chapter 7

She felt so guilty, but she knew she had to leave him.

Flossy knew what she would have been up against - four Bovine assassins; she recognized the trade mark take down from her training days. There was no way she could face off against four killer cows: that would only have resulted in her being one big fluffy, black and white pancake. Absolutely no good to anybody.

The last thing she wanted to do was abandon her master, it hurt her to do so, but there was nothing she physically could have done to help him once those monsters had sprung their trap.

However, Flossy still couldn't believe he'd fallen for it; that stupid boy.

But that was Jimmy, wasn't it – always thinking about others before himself. That was one of the things she loved most about him. He had cared for her all these years and never asked for anything in return except her companionship. Even though the pair had been thrown together under orders from her superiors, she had never once regretted the assignment due to the bond they had forged over time, developing into a deep friendship.

It pained her as she remembered the look of anguish in his eyes as she had turned away from him as he lay under the big fat cow. But she'd been helpless.

Flossy, thinking fast and acting on her training, had decided to make a quick exit, take some time to reformulate a plan and then hurry to save her friend. She was fairly sure that the cows were not going to kill him, they could have done that there and then, she'd recognised they only wanted to capture him and that gave her a little time.

However, she was sure this wouldn't be long.

Once the Bovines figured out what they were dealing with, they would dispose of him for sure. But worse still, they would discover the only weakness in their plans, know how to identify it and, worse than that, how to counter and obliterate it.

She couldn't stop them on her own, just one against hundreds, Flossy needed help.

Now was the time to put all her years of training into action and call upon the assistance of a race of beasts that, with their aged wisdom and countless experience of dealing with the Bovines, could help in this situation.

She would call upon the aid of 'The Masters'.

Flossy had already perceived some evidence that they had been helping Jimmy along the way, influencing him as their human aid, so she decided to put that theory to the test.

Calling upon her lifelong skill and the innate ability of her breed, it was time to do what she had been put on these green pastures to do.

She just hoped *they* were feeling co-operative.

It would not be an easy journey to reach them though as the canine had to cross a cow infested village before reaching the path to the country headquarters in the base of the hills - a long distance for a dog.

On sneaking away from the entrapment Flossy had managed to get herself to the rear of the doctor's house and was hiding behind a low wall that bordered the drive where Dr Healsnaught kept his car.

Belly to the floor, her ears whipped round scanning the vicinity like a pair of radar satellite dishes trying to pick up any hint of pursuit or covert hoof-fall. Her nose was in overdrive, sucking the air like a spasmodic vacuum cleaner trying to detect the scent of any potential hostile Bovine, although most of the time you don't need a hyper sensitive canine nose to smell one.

A settled calm had taken hold now and deliberately slowing her breathing, she focused her keen senses analysing the quiet surroundings and all scents associated with them upon the warm gentle breeze.

Still no bird song, they were on silent running, which was good as it meant the Avians were still on high alert. No other animals around either; most of them obviously wanting to remain neutral in this conflict. Probably a good idea, although it did surprise her that she hadn't seen any cats around. Those vigilante opportunists usually revelled in situations like this, always trying to twist a crisis to their own ends or just for sheer malice; those twisted felines. She would have to keep an eye out for them.

After several long concentrated minutes of intense observation, Flossy was satisfied she was alone. Now all she had to do was make it to the foothills of the valley on the far side of Farmer Ken's farm.

It was a route she knew well, as she and Jimmy had spent a lot of time there during their sheep herding training. Or, at least, what passed for training, as Jimmy would shout instructions and animatedly blow his whistle a lot, whilst she usually ignored him and strolled around as she pleased. Luckily the sheep, who she knew well, were a helpful bunch and would herd themselves through the gates just to get the whole thing over with.

It was normally an easy pleasant walk across the village.

Not now though. Things were going to be a little different.

This time it meant she would be travelling straight through cow central.

Flossy had no doubt that, en route, she would meet other blotchy leatherheads as well and by the now the clever canine was sure that an alert would have gone out issuing order to search out and destroy the black and white dog that had been aiding the strange young human boy.

Flossy began weighing up her current options.

She could go route one, as fast as her four legs could carry her, through open enemy territory. This however was a risky strategy, simply due to the cows' numbers; they would easily spot her and even with her speed advantage she would just struggle to outmanoeuvre the sheer masses and would eventually tire.

Another course of action would be ultimate stealth. A safer strategy of course, but much slower and she couldn't afford to waste any more time; not with her young master's life in the balance.

Flossy concluded to herself that it would have to be a combination of both and then improvise on any situations that were put before her as they arose.

Lifting herself from the floor in determination, she gave herself a little nod as she mentally determined and plotted her route.

One last big sniff of the air just to be sure; she momentarily froze.

Quickly she looked round.

There was nothing there.

Another big sniff.

Strange.

Flossy shook her head; she must have been mistaken.

She was almost certain she caught the scent of…something familiar, but there was no-one around.

In resignation but with extreme caution, the shaggy black and white sheepdog pointed her nose in the direction she wanted to go and began to follow it.

Concealed in a high branch in a nearby tree, two slitted amber green eyes followed her departure.

A calculating fanged grin spread below long white whiskers.

A fleeting black shadow nimbly hopped down from branch to branch before landing with great agility and grace on the garage roof. Hugging the shade, keeping downwind, following the oblivious canine, it began its journey of stealth intent on mischief.

Meanwhile, soaring above the rooftops, a little brown and red flash was taking on board everything it had just observed outside the doctor's house. Its little red feathered chest was heaving with the exertion it was using to fly as fast as its little wings could carry it.

Adrian the robin was also on its way to 'The Masters' with urgent in the field information that was critical to the campaign.

Adrian? A robin? That seems quite a normal name you might think. You see, it is common knowledge among birds that robins are never called by any name that begins with an 'R'. Historically, they got fed up being called by the popular 'R' related boys name (especially the females) so long ago, it was decided that all names beginning with R would be dropped from the Avian language altogether. It is also believed that the Thrush population also wanted to replace their name, but it never happened as it was understood that the alternative they proposed, Itchy, would never work.

The stupid human boy had been caught; they would want to know immediately and that was Adrian's mission.

Adrian had soon cleared the perimeter of the Golthwaite observing, as he flew past, the lines of people all gently swaying in a strange wavelike unison and blocking off all the entry and exit routes around the village.

Human shields, he surmised. *Clever.*

Any human assistance from outside the village would be forced to go through their own kind; something, the robin knew, the humans would be unwilling to do. They would never hurt their own species intentionally.

Each group of people was being directed by a small selection of cows, always in close proximity. Adrian counted groups of four of them every so often. They were obviously the troops directing the front lines. Although they were spread a little thinly here and there, they appeared to be covering a huge telepathic range and close enough with one another to form a mental link keeping them in touch with headquarters.

More intelligence to report back to The Masters.

Banking a sharp left to set his course better against sudden gust of breeze, he knew that not only would he highly visible against the clear blue sky, but the cows could mark his passing quite easily; he was now the only bird up here. All his colleagues must have gone to ground awaiting orders or further instruction.

Luckily for him, the Bovines seemed quite intent on the task at hand directing and controlling the human folk and none of them had looked upwards yet. The little robin was flying at high risk but seemed to be getting away with it, hidden in plain view.

Raising his altitude slightly to see beyond a small copse of trees near the stream, his desired location in the foothills of the Dales, just at the opening of a V shaped valley, came into view.

From this height and distance what looked like a large collection of cotton wool balls appeared to be converging on the stream's source that meandered its course from that valley onto the dale below, thus forming a soft cloudy mattress in the fields; as if someone had put bubble bath in the spring.

He had found The Masters.

Taking a few more sharp breaths, he tucked in his wings and dived bombed his way towards the floor cloud.

Now all he had to do was pick out the one known as Mop.

Flossy, trying to get to the same location as Adrian, was finding the route there a little more taxing. Down every street or lane that she turned, she seemed to find herself facing either a wall of wobbly tranced humans holding hands and swaying from side to side reminiscent of a peaceful hippy protest or an eager eyed Bovine patrolling the vicinity on the lookout for trouble from any would be heroes or problematic homosapiens.

Flossy was still unsure if the alert had gone out to be wary of any black and white sheepdogs, but was sure they'd work it out sooner or later that, if seen, she would not be on their side.

At this moment, the enterprising collie was hidden behind some dustbins studying the blockade of eight humans and three cows that were barring her desired exit out of the village. This route would lead to the valley opening and the path running beside the stream that would get her there.

But where was the fourth cow? They always worked in quads and only three were visible. That was a potential problem.

On either side of these human and bovine obstacles were two pretty little stone cottages covered in climbing roses surrounded by mossy three foot high walls that bordered the road creating a bottleneck.

Only one way in, one way out; the cows had done their research.

Going around would take far too long so that was not an option.

Flossy looked out from behind the bins surveying the garden she was in. It was at the back of a family house, she guessed, looking at all the outdoor toys that were strewn around on the lawn and patio. A ball here, a bike discarded over there and a well worn red and yellow plastic slide on rather well worn and patchy grass.

The owners obviously weren't at home either, as the house doors lay wide open. Probably under Bovine control, maybe even part of the group blocking the road ahead.

Flossy was scanning for anything useful, when her eager eyes landed on two pairs of pink children's wellington boots just stood outside the back door.

A cunning plan began to form, but she would need something else to complete the ruse.

A little more searching and she found what she needed; a child's pink plastic football of the ninety nine pence blow away variety.

This was risky as, of course, she would never fool the cows with what she was about to attempt but with a little misdirection, the unthinking humans might just be duped.

The only other things she needed now were a lot of guts and a whole mountain full of luck.

Carefully Flossy positioned the pink wellies, which were very small, and probably belonging to a pair of infants, with her mouth in to pairs, one behind the other, then lifting her legs, placed her paws in them. They were just tight enough so that when she walked they didn't fall off.

She then positioned the plastic ball between her legs and with her jaw and teeth began to squeeze.

Pop!

She swung her head around anxiously to make sure she had no observers and drawn any attention to herself with the loud noise. Luckily, after several deep breaths, she realised she had gotten away with it.

So far, so good.

So the clever collie picked up the now floppy pink plastic and arranged it with her mouth over her snout.

The black and white dog now appeared to have a big pink nose and big pink feet and was trying very hard to look like, yes…a cow (or perhaps a calf).

She could pass for a one of *them*, she surmised, to those who were half blind and standing at a distance of around half a mile away, stood behind a wall and had also never seen a cow before, but she didn't have time to worry about that now.

Before setting off, she caught a glimpse of herself in the patio doors. The absolute futility of her plan momentarily dawned upon her. Thinking she must be mad to be carrying on with this charade she began plodding her way out through the garden gate and down the street towards the barricade.

Meanwhile, something streamlined and black slithered in her wake, just on the edge of awareness.

Momentarily the hairs on Flossy's scruff tingled and she nervously looked around.

Again there was nothing there.

With great uncertainty, she continued; her tummy now turning somersaults.

She was about to come into the visual range of the Bovines, who just seemed to be chatting amongst themselves for the moment as they were arranged in a triangle all looking at one another and none of them in Flossy's direction.

Flossy needed a distraction quick or this would never work and for the first time began to panic.

The cows down the street were indeed talking with one another.

"Do you think my rump looks big today?" One of them asked the other two.

"Oh yes," another replied. "Would make a fine steak, would that."

The third one started laughing, momentarily allowing her concentration to wander from the swaying humans. This allowed a young man to become detached from the line, who then start ambling down the road towards one of the three foot garden walls, one of which he then proceeded to walk straight into therefore falling over it face first into the owners rhubarb patch.

At once the three Bovines turned to see what caused such a calamity and went to investigate, one of them looking a little bashful.

"Ooh, quick. Get him back before the commander returns or she'll have our leather for handbags." Three concerned heads lifted themselves over the wall to peer at the stricken human.

Heart beating a drum roll in her chest, Flossy saw her chance.

Sneaking along behind the sidetracked squad, as best she could in plastic pink wellies, she shuffled up to the swaying line where she was met by seven confused faces examining her intently with interrogating eyes, almost as if they were waiting for her to say something. However they didn't immediately react negatively which was a good start.

The stand off lasted seconds, but it felt like hours to Flossy. She had to do something before those cows turned round to refocus on their task.

"Moo-f!" she barked quietly, trying the best cow impersonation she could muster.

Nothing happened.

"Moo-f! She tried again.

To her surprise this seemed to satisfy the folk before her, acting almost as if they'd met an old friend and was pleased to help them out, and they parted at the middle beckoning her through.

She'd done it.

Gaining a small amount of confidence, she ambled her way through (again as quickly as she could in the wellies) and the human barrier closed behind her.

Phew, that wasn't too bad, she thought, quite easy really and slowly she continued on her way knowing that the back of those human heads weren't watching her and her appearance would be blocked from the view of the cows by now.

Once completely out of sight she could remove her ridiculous disguise and set off at haste to meet The Masters.

Suddenly, out of the quiet calm, came the loudest screeching, screaming, wailing meow that was ever produced, freezing Flossy agonizingly to the spot.

Heart pumping twofold again, Flossy turned around and there, between the legs of a human woman in the middle of the line with an arched back and an impossibly large grin on its face was a smug looking black cat.

Flossy's eyes narrowed on the feline tormentor, the strange feeling she'd had earlier now tangible before her eyes, emitting cold malice. But then they were drawn away beyond it to see three pairs of glassy round black eyes staring back with furious intent framed by beautifully fluttering eyelashes.

Placing the worst canine curse on the cat, Flossy realised she'd been rumbled.

Pure, animal instinct took over.

Rearing onto hind legs and with a frantic flurry of her front legs she released her paws from the pink wellies and then spinning herself round, her back end facing the cat, she whipped her hind legs into the air like a bronking buck, firing the remaining wellies rapidly straight into the face of the no longer grinning moggy, sending it sprawling onto its back and under the hooves of the now advancing cows.

Her satisfaction was short lived as she knew she had to get away fast.

Flossy spat the fake nose down to the floor and it wasn't until this point that the forcibly dim witted humans realised that she wasn't a cow. Their faces became so bent in a twisted rage that she didn't think was capable of a lovely human and a mighty roar of 'moos' erupted from them.

They weren't the only ones that seemed bent upon revenge at the deceit, the cows faces were flushing with anger and were quickly relaying mental commands at the people before them. However, you didn't have to be a mind reader to know what they were instructing.

Flossy didn't hang around to find out either. Spinning around again she shot off into the nearest hedgerow she could find trying to put an immediate barrier between her and the now rapidly moving humans that were now intent upon her capture.

That was her first mistake.

Once through the brambly entanglement she was immediately cut off by the stream that was in front of her. At this point, in a lower part of the streams course, it was quite wide, deep and fast moving and, worst of all, had no part of it that was crossable. She had originally planned to cross at the old pack horse bridge further upstream.

Flossy stood, nose to the water, panting with anxiety wondering how she was ever going to get across to escape her tormentors. Trying to swim across at this point, with current as it was, would only carry her downstream and further away from her intended destination, back into the centre of the village and back amongst the now alerted herd.

The village folk were now unceremoniously crashing their way straight through the hedge, regardless of the tearing of their clothes and skin by the snagging branches and brambles, heedless to the pain it was causing them as all they wanted to do was obey their masters instructions and 'get that dog'.

They were nearly through.

Flossy had to act.

The humans were right behind her advancing very quickly, too quickly.

Despite their mind controlled status the anger and urgency of the cows was being transmitted with alarming strength and that was translating into very fast action, if a little clumsy.

Three of the humans were sprinting towards her with wild abandon; it would be difficult for them to halt their charge. Flossy's quick mind sprang into action and readied her lithe finely tuned canine prowess.

The lead human, a middle aged athletic looking chap, was first to reach her and dived without thought trying to snatch the dog quickly within his grasp.

He clutched the air before sliding down the wet bank and straight into the stream face first taking in a large mouthful of water as he did.

Unwittingly, the two remaining villagers, a young girl and possibly her mother judging from their vague similarities in badly applied make-up, were too close behind and became tangled in one another, succumbing to the same fate as the first gentleman who received a second dunking as the slap faced pair landed upon him in a huge splash.

Flossy, in a mind boggling flash of speed had simply jumped to the side at the last possible moment, therefore catching the hapless three off guard and bungling towards the chilly water with no ability to stop.

There was no time to enjoy this small victory as the other four villagers were now quickly advancing through the thicket.

Then the opportunity presented itself.

The water may have been too deep for a sheep dog, but the three wading humans were now stooped over in the stream only up their midriffs.

With no time to spare, Flossy exploded into action, veering for the floundered three with her best speed. She bunched her muscles and sprang from the waters edge landing between the shoulders of the man, who was spouting water from his mouth with a big spurt whilst exhaling a big "umph", and then vaulting from there to the opposite shore.

With this, the man again lost his footing on the slippery underwater rocks, bundled into the mascara running ugly sisters resulting in the three bobbing under the water and being swept away by the current a short distance downstream.

Flossy stood facing them from the opposite shore where the other four people were mooing at her with angry visages, but were obviously hesitant in entering the water.

She'd bought herself some time.

Now on the correct side of the stream, she could soon join up with the path she intended to follow.

As she set on her way, she could hear from behind the splashes and shouts of humans as they were delayed by the stream.

A mighty "mooooooo" chorus erupted into the air; it was edged with frustration, anger but most of all despair. The cows were not happy.

Allowing herself a little mental smile, Flossy padded off at best speed along the bank of the stream, following its course that would lead to the spring at its source.

Hopefully she hadn't lost too much time.

Action may be taken soon...

"There hasn't been a gathering like this in some time."

"Indeed, there hasn't."

"But this is a desperate time."

"The Avians report the village perimeter has been secured and all incoming humans are succumbing."

"The guardian has vanished and the emissary is captured. These are dire times."

"When do we act?"

"Based on current information we dare not interfere yet. We need word from the guardian."

"We must be called upon to act; we cannot intercede of our own will."

"Let us pray that she arrives soon, then."

"Good, now let's move apart a bit. Between us we must have the insulative qualities of a quilt and I'm starting to get a bit sweaty."

Chapter 8

The first thing he became aware of was that smell clinging right to the back of his throat. The thick, musky odour of hay, cow muck and earthy sweaty animals assaulted his nostrils. Having worked on the farm for some time Jimmy considered himself familiar with the 'Parfum de Farmyard' but this assault on his sinuses was unbelievable. This place hadn't been mucked out for quite some time. They may control humans, but it seemed they neglected themselves when it came to hygiene.

As perception of his surroundings grew, though his eyes were still closed, his ears were greeted by a glitz of botty bellows; he was finding it quite difficult to breathe the musty air.

Something was very close.

Gradually getting his wits about him, he tried to move to get a better feel for his surroundings but on trying to raise himself, his wrists unexpectedly burned and chafed. On further inspection he found they were tied to a timber post within a cow stall. Goodness knows how the cows had managed to tie a knot, having no fingers at all, but never the less it had been achieved

Gingerly, he opened his eyes.

He gasped in astonishment as he was faced with three cows staring straight back at him, no further than a couple of metres away, ominous silhouettes against the sunlight that crept in through various cracks like laser beams through a dust cloud.

It appeared as if they were studying him.

Studying him very hard.

Jimmy could swear they had slightly furrowed brows and were squinting in concentration and they were shaking slightly they seemed to be trying that hard – at something. It was similar to the expression you might get if you asked a six year old to solve a quadratic equation and explain it to you in Greek.

After what seemed a few, long, silent, unbearable, impatient, uncertain, tense…… moments his Bovine captors appeared to almost get bored, yet frustrated, with what they were doing; shaking their heads in a negative fashion. Turning their backs on him, they formed a small huddle.

Jimmy couldn't believe what his eyes were seeing – he could almost swear they were conferring. Occasionally, one of them would turn their head towards him, perform a quick examination and then turn back again or they would look towards one another and nod in a comical bobbing fashion. If Jimmy didn't know better, he could almost believe they were having a full conversation; but none of them were making any noise.

What was going on? Jimmy thought to himself, both curious of the situation yet fearful of his predicament.

His eyes investigated further into the sun cracked gloom.

He realised he was alone; no other humans. No Flossy. Just surrounded by cows. Tens of cows. Hundreds of cows. His situation dawned on him like unwanted diarrhoea. His fear violated his buttocks. *Parp!*

The last few moments before his capture came into his mind, revisiting the last faint memories, the vague shadows, before his lapse in unconsciousness. He wished he hadn't as once again he became overwhelmed by the feelings of hurt and betrayal caused by Flossy's abandonment. Never ever would he have believed that she would leave his side; she was his faithful shadow, his right arm, the butter to his bread, the pie to his peas.

Not any more.

Jimmy felt empty and alone with no idea of how he got into, or indeed how he would get out of, this pitiful mess and wondered if he could even be bothered to try.

Giving himself a mental slap and pulling himself together, the young lad began to ponder the situation he was in. *Why did they want him anyway? Why had they captured him? Why was he so special? Why did they always seem to be studying him?*

As long as he'd been helping out on Ken's farm he had never seen any inkling of this behaviour before, they had hidden it well. He reluctantly applauded their clever deception. Every day they had been led down to the milking shed, always following each other and being herded along never showing anything more than a desire for a good feed. No sign of resistance had ever been displayed, they were always so docile. It was obviously all a brilliant façade to keep their human keepers oblivious to their plans. They must have been very patient he thought.

By now Jimmy had identified that, in his present location, he was unlikely to be found by anyone. Mr and Mrs Farmer Ken were both in a trance and nobody else would be visiting the farm today as it was the weekend.

Looking round he began to evaluate his options. Aware of his responsibility to the village he knew he had to escape, rally some sort of defensive force or get word outside Golthwaite and then combat this Bovine threat. He decided he'd work on that part later; the first part of that plan, escaping, would be hard enough.

The mantle of would-be hero was now on Jimmy's shoulders.

His parents would have been proud to know that their Jimmy had found his calling in life, even if he wasn't doing that well at the moment.

Scanning the buildings dimly lit interior, as cows can't operate light switches, Jimmy could see several cows in stalls being milked by the machine – willingly, with no humans to usher them in. Surely, he thought, this would still require somebody to operate the equipment so, he surmised, somebody must be about at least to operate the machinery although they were probably under the cows' control. Jimmy made a mental note to seek out that person as they may potentially be an ally or if they were under the control of the cows, maybe he could help them.

The machinery was operating at full capacity and judging from the storage levels, had been for some time.

Jimmy had never seen milk production on this scale before. There were gallons upon gallons of the hideous stuff; it was almost as if they'd been holding it back just for this occasion.

Jimmy then noticed that the three cows that were studying him earlier were now wandering around, separate from the main herd, casually inspecting things as they moved about, still looking to be in conference. Occasionally, other cows would walk up to these three, this official trio would stare at it, nod or shake their heads and then the cow would tootle off disappearing from the shed either on their own or taking a few companions with them. This was all very unusual, yet organised and civil behaviour. Very similar to how a military base of operations may perform in the movies Jimmy had seen.

Every now and again, one of those three would pass his way and cast a glance at him with narrowed eyes and furrowed brow. Luckily, these visits were rather infrequent so Jimmy realised they mustn't be guarding him. They arrogantly believed, now they had him tied up, he was no longer a threat to them.

The ingenious youngster aimed to prove them wrong, seeing this as an opportunity to escape. If only he could just untie his bonds he could probably sneak out unnoticed amongst the stalls, machinery, feed, hay and distracted beasts.

Better still, if he could make his way to the milking machines controls or storage vessels, he could enact Flossy's plan of destroying and ridding themselves of gallons of milk and their ability to extract it at the source. All Jimmy needed to do was get access to the suction machinery, this being probably the best opportunity to create chaos, or even the storage vessels as, destroying either of these could stall the cows' plans for a while by cutting off the supply network.

This could possibly free some of the villagers from control just long enough to put together some form of defensive resistance or at least summon official help; the police, the army, anyone.

Jimmy was chuffed with himself for being able to formulate these plans, even though his head was still buzzing slightly. Contemplating his woolly cap, he thought *I wonder if I can get more of these? They may come in handy.*

Back to the problem of Jimmy freeing himself first. Testing the strength of the rope that tied his hands again he found there was no give. The bonds were so tight that, with every little move, they chaffed and dug into his wrists a little bit more. Jimmy winced. Also, the timber post that the rope was looped around was also firmly in place, there would be no way of moving that.

The situation suddenly became hopeless again and Jimmy's fear started to re-awaken. Unable to move, he was surrounded by four legged black and white beasts and worst of all it didn't look like they were going to feed him either and it was nearly lunchtime – unless they were going to give him milk. Yuck! The young lad shuddered at the mere thought of consuming anything liquid and white; there was no chance he would be drinking that stuff.

Also, with the villagers all under the influence of the cows' mind control, who would be left to save him should he become affected by their powers?

Feeling thoroughly deflated and miserable, he sat amongst the muck and straw sulking over his predicament.

Jimmy sank lower and lower towards despair, when suddenly he was amazed to see Mrs Farmer Ken wander out from behind the milking machine and begin to robotically tend the cows in their stalls. *How long had she been there?* Nishi had adopted the now familiar staggering walking style of the undead which looked even more comical in her striped pink pyjamas and an increasingly dirty pair of fluffy pink slippers. Her long black hair still had the 'got out of bed' look, halfway between static electricity shock and a force five gale, and her heavy lidded angled eyes were vacant, her face expressionless.

"Mrs Farmer Ken!" Jimmy whispered as loud as he dared. "Over here! Please help. It's me Jimmy."

"Moo?" she answered inquisitively, her eyes squinted in his direction.

"Over here, in this stall. I'm tied up. Please, help."

"Moo? Moo? Miiillk."

Jimmy sagged. "Oh no, she's still affected. I should never have left her, thought she would have been safe in her bedroom."

"Moo!" The farmer's wife suddenly stood erect, eyes widening rapidly and focusing on Jimmy, and raised her arm pointing at the young prisoner. "Moo! Moo! Moo!"

Rather spookily, in complete unison, the cows' heads and eyes followed the line of Nishi's finger and began to scrutinise the shrinking Jimmy. After briefly looking to one another, they seemed to reach some sort of decision. This led to the young lad becoming a little more than apprehensive as he began to feel even more vulnerable in his captive state.

What Jimmy could only describe as the 'lead' cow, the checker board one, slowly wandered up to him with a menacing swagger as though on a fashion runway, stepping up face to face with him, noses almost touching, then let out a huge snort of contempt causing Jimmy to cringe as he received a snotty face of which the nasal contents began dripping from his chin.

The black and white adversary then proceeded to rotate itself through one hundred and eighty degrees placing its substantial rump directly in Jimmy's face.

This did not bode well.

It was not good as no-one ever wanted to be in a position where they have to look at a cow's behind, with the exception of vets of course, but they are paid to do such things.

Lifting its tail, the cow went rigid; seeming to brace itself before a mighty gaseous discharge erupted enveloping the young lad, almost blasting the sinuses from his nose and through the back of his head. Tears were streaming from the stinging in his eyes, the scent virtually peeling off the corneas from within his grotesquely tortured head, his ears popping with the change in air pressure.

It was too much....once again Jimmy entered the land of nod.

After some considerable time, Jimmy strolled his way back into the land of the conscious carrying with him a head full of fog. His predicament certainly hadn't improved and he was feeling a lot worse than he was before, physically, mentally and a little nauseas actually. Unsurprisingly, his last remaining reserves of resolve were fading fast.

As his gaze contemplated the muck strewn floor beneath him, something small suddenly caught his attention out of the corner of his eye; a little flicker of movement heading his way, barely nudging the straw that it was shoving its way through.

With amazement he realised what it was – a robin, the very same one he had seen that morning. Although they all do look very similar Jimmy had a good eye for these things.

As memories of their previous meeting returned Jimmy started to feel a complete idiot for not heeding the warning of the red chested harbinger of trouble. A big clicking sound registered within his head as pieces were now starting to fit together; Well it's not every day a robin tries to talk to you – how was he supposed to understand the message?

The little bundle of red and brown feathers focused its glossy black beads up at the prone teenager sat in the stall almost with a look of 'I told you so' on its beaky face. Which is very difficult for a tiny bird as you will appreciate the Avian species have not really developed the facial qualities and dexterity required to portray such complex emotion.

In this case though, as an avid observer and fond admirer of the human species, this feathery visitor was feeling sorry for this stricken young lad and had decided to help. It had also had orders from The Masters that should this boy need aid it should be given and this bird was willing to do anything for the cause.

The robin also felt he owed something to the kind humans for leaving out all those seeds, nuts and greasy fat balls over the winter time, although he would still have to work off the gut he had developed after those lardy treats.

Jimmy watched curiously as the little robin hopped along the floor and disappeared behind his back. A few moments later he could feel the rope around his wrist loosening.

Amazing.

Jimmy quickly looked towards the cows to make sure they weren't watching or at least noticed the little visitor. This was an unexpected but delightful turn of events and the last thing he wanted to do was risk discovery of his avian friend. His eyes and nostrils were still burning with the after tang from his last encounter with a cow's rear end and that was an experience he didn't want repeated.

With a sudden hint of suspicion, one of the cows looked over and began scrutinizing him. Instantly Jimmy began to feign grogginess and let out small moans and groans in an attempt to mislead his watcher into believing he was still incapacitated and under the gaseous effects. Luckily, this seemed to work as the cow appeared satisfied with what it saw. All the while his bonds were becoming increasing slacker.

The young lad patiently bided his time knowing he would soon be free.

On the other side of the shed, Patch was becoming increasingly agitated.

She was nervous, she was vexed and her hide seemed to stretch a little tighter over her bulky frame than normal.

"What's taking so long? I've received reports back from units three, six and eight, all with good news. They each have a collective herd of humans under their control, securing the village perimeter to the south east and north, easy enough with minimal resistance.

Unit one, Daisy's elite unit, has apprehended the problem male youth," she glanced around to the far end to see Jimmy still on the floor emitting groans, hands still tied behind his back and his head lolling too and fro, "but we're yet to ascertain what he knows. Remaining units are taking far too long. Do we have any other news? Her

Horn-ness will be expecting a report shortly; I don't want to disappoint her. "

"Ma'am, units two and seven did have the furthest distance to travel, just out of telepathic range, and reports state that the humans under the influence of mind control of groups reporting in are losing some of their basic motor skills, an unforeseen side effect, leading to an increased time to move them to their desired positions." Clover, as always by Patch's side, updated the commander as units advised their status through the communication network.

She continued, "We are also experiencing some other unexpected symptoms to our cerebral control formulation. It seems the humans are encountering larger than usual cravings for our milk based products, therefore leading to distraction. I have hypothesized that this is how the human boy managed to lure the farmer away." Clover continued collating the field reports as they came in from the 'cows in the field'. "It appears we've had a report from unit eight of humans taking pints from doorsteps and a report from unit five of another human splinter group apparently, and I quote, 'chasing a cheese'."

"It's not good enough! Why were these results not found in initial testing? Someone is going to answer for that." Patch mused. Clover blanched slightly. "Issue the order to increase haste towards mission objectives at once. Use force, mental or physical if necessary. I want the village secure by dusk to prove to the High Longhorn that such a feat can be accomplished in the required timescale. Outside human agencies will be starting to merge on the village, raising their suspicions as to why no-one is responding to them or even returning to them and we can't have that, otherwise the greater mission will be aborted and we will be held accountable.

I don't mind admitting that I do not want to be at the receiving end of the Divine Bovine's wrath should we fail. She will not be merciful." Patch visibly trembled at the thought. "I heard reports that the last herd that failed her were left *un-milked*– a fate I do not wish to share."

Exactly as it sounds, being un-milked is a very painful and sometimes explosive way for a cow to go. It is said the popping sound can be heard for miles.

Clover closed her eyes contemplating this and her black Patches almost went grey at the thought. She quickly changed the subject, "We must also be ready to defend our position against other forces. The human perimeter will act as a shield against any weaponry they bring against us. To cause any damage they will have to either send in foot soldiers or bomb us from afar. I seriously doubt they would be willing to kill their own with long range artillery under the threat of cows and any soldiers coming into range will easily be within reach of our mind control before they can do any harm."

"Daisy, front and centre soldier." Patch called out.

"Yes Ma'am," came a voice from among the throng.

"Dispatch the order to increase speed on all issued orders, add extra troops to the despatched squads if required. Use some of the milkers if needed. I want reports of completion within the hour. Don't let me down."

"I will kick some rump to up the rate of urgency, Ma'am. I will threaten a flame grill to anyone's sirloin who does not comply."

"Ok, Ok. Very good Daisy. Dismissed."

As Daisy plodded off to mentally relay orders, Patch said to Clover, "I am pleased with that cow's performance during this operation. Make sure she and her squad receive a commendation for her efforts, especially for the young human capture." It was a good job she hadn't heard about the zebra crossing incident!

"Yes Ma'am, of course. She did an excellent job in capturing the renegade boy. She may be a little contrary at times, but her methods will never cease to amaze me."

Orders issued and satisfied her herd would carry them out, Patch now turned her attention back towards the conundrum of the young farm hand Daisy had apprehended, allowing herself another moment to study him a little more closely. She still couldn't tap into his brain and that alone was worrying her. Why couldn't she read his thoughts? Even sense a small amount of emotion? It was not only that, but she couldn't even register any activity there at all. Very disturbing as, physically speaking, he should be dead.

What she had come to recognise is that if the humans were to form any sort of resistance, this is the form it would take, and she was not going to let a bunch of brain-dead homosapiens ruin their plans to conquer the world.

After further scrutiny, eyeing him from head to toe, Patch's apprehension grew at the clothing he was found to be wearing. That was a lot of woollen wear and that hat looked ridiculous.

Another hand had been dealt in this game and the extra player was trying to remain anonymous. However, Patch, drawing upon her years of experience, was certain they had encountered this enemy before. There were familiar patterns and it was beginning to trouble her that they were willing to interfere in this way, so indirectly and on the side of the humans. That fact alone repulsed her. She had never understood their fondness for the pink hairless flesh bags.

Patch wondered how much more they knew. To plot a counter measure like this must have taken a long time preparing so she guessed they were quite well informed.

Understanding dawned.

They are aware of our plans.

She had seen enough, extra urgency set in.

This threat ended now.

Turning back to her sub-ordinates she issued the terrible order, "Dispose of that boy immediately. Then find any more like him and get rid of them too. We will not let this unknown element stand in our way. The Ovies Aries are involved and we must quash this threat now."

As the cows caught Patch's telepathic thoughts, moos of approval erupted around the cow shed.

Jimmy could physically feel the sudden change in mood around him, the atmosphere becoming suddenly tense. Essences of meanness, menace and malice were exuding from the cow that had just been examining him, that big patchwork one, and there was certainly an evil look in that one's eyes. No need for telepathy to determine that.

Sudden desperation forced him to act; it was either now or never as a dark circle was beginning to form around him, his means of escape rapidly decreasing. The only exit was quickly disappearing behind a screen of dirty hooves and knobbly knees.

The little robin had miraculously freed his hands without the cows even being aware, so he was no longer attached to the stall post. Fingers were tingling as they began to regain their feeling. You may be surprised how strong robins are but, of course, you must remember robins are territorial so they are always up for a bit of a scrap. The robin beak boxing league puts those namby pamby human wrestlers to shame.

In a brief moment, before the black and white blotched oppressors were close enough to apprehend him again, Jimmy took in a deep breath to steady his nerves (and to brace against any more gas attacks) and with bunched muscles and lightening speed, he made his move.

In encouragement, the robin had hopped up on to his shoulder, commanding a position of authority and issuing enthusiastic chirps as they left the dirty floor and made a beeline through a tight gap amongst the motley crew toward the side of the cowshed where the milking machine was situated, which quite conveniently was also adjacent to the exit, something that also might be quite useful considering the circumstances.

All feelings of fear had now evaporated from the young lad to be replaced by a fierce determination, strong will and courage spurring him into incredible bravery. It now became clear to him that he was now willing to do anything to stop these Bovine aggressors. They would rue the day they let rip in his face.

Shocked moos of alarm rang amongst the stalls.

Cows clumsily moved in urgency in an attempt to intercept this young human rebel, but in the gloom of the sheds interior they either stumbled against each other or even more comically, as they were restrained by the milking tubes attached to their udders, performed a hilarious parade of cow bungee.

"Stop him!" ordered Patch, seeing the catastrophe unfolding around her.

Ducking and weaving amongst the calamitous cattle, Jimmy reached his objective, the big glugging, whining and clunking milking machine.

Only to be confronted by Mrs Farmer Ken.

The look on her face was quite disturbing; it was a mixture of confusion, pain and anger framed by wild unkempt bed hair that flew al over the place at rather jaunty angles. The baby pink of the pyjamas did nothing to soften it.

What he didn't know was the amount of Bovine brainwaves assaulting her grey matter was resulting in a conflict that her mind that could not comprehend. She was undergoing synaptic overload as, in a panic, every cow in the shed was trying to mentally instruct her at once as the only human available.

Momentarily she staggered on the spot, swaying haphazardly from side to side, her eyes crossing in the middle, then suddenly she froze, became erect, the pupils in her eyes sharpening to pin pricks and began to take on a sinister air.

Her vision finally focused on Jimmy.

Jimmy stopped in his tracks fearing for his friend, trying to read her intentions.

Patch's focus and concentration intensified on the Japanese farmwife taking authority over all those other voices in her head imparting devious commands of a 'none too pleasant' nature.

"Attack, Kill, Destroy. Do my bidding."

Nishi robotically scanned her surroundings and eyes settling upon a stout metal bucket, she picked it up holding it menacingly in her right hand. A sneer curled its way on to her lips and her eyes slanted even narrower to the point they almost looked closed.

She arranged her stance into the crouch of the tiger. Jimmy quickly glanced around nervously.

Slowly but surely, Nishi's arm began a slow rotation, building slowly, around and around in a windmill motion swinging the bucket around her in a martial arts fashion. Over one shoulder, then the other, switching from hand to hand with a precision and accuracy that was distinctly martial arts. She flailed the pail around as if it was the Japanese farmer's weapon of choice.

Jimmy's eyes widened realising what was coming.

Mrs Farmer Ken advanced stealthily surrounded by now a silver blur, a low moaning screechy noise issuing from deep within her throat.

"Mrs Farmer Ken! Nishi! Stop. Please stop," Jimmy did not want to harm her or indeed be harmed by her. He waved his arms out in front of him, trying to deter her away. The robin gripped on for dear life, luckily his little feet getting a good grip on Jimmy's woolly top.

Cautiously he backed away, tiny shuffling steps, one foot after the other, head furiously searching the room for a safe way out of this mess whilst all the time staying out of the reach of that menacing pail of death.

It was too late; he felt the cold stone and warm metal on his back as he was corralled into the corner in between the rough stone shed wall and the machinery.

Trapped.

Nishi was getting closer. Jimmy didn't know what to do.

The milking machinery behind him, a bucket wielding maniac bearing down in front of him and behind her a mass of black and white with fiery eyes relishing the coming onslaught resulting in the boys ultimate demise.

Quite honestly, it wasn't looking good for young Jimmy. The odds of escaping were as slim as a camel going skiing.

The little robin, who had amazingly stayed with Jimmy up till this point, seemed to recognise the impending outcome. It turned its head to look at the doomed youth with an apologetic look in its eyes, let out a pitiful chirp of apology and gave another one of those little shoulder shrugs before launching itself into the rafters out of harms way. Only morbid curiosity prevented it from leaving, he would of course have to report this back.

Once again, Jimmy's heart fell realising that for the second time today he had been abandoned when he needed help the most.

Taking all these facts into consideration, to say things were looking a bit grim at that moment would be an understatement but Jimmy remarkably became quite calm about his situation. He looked around to assess the options, an aura of acceptance descending on him. Time appeared to slow before his eyes.

Although backed up against a large piece of technical equipment he knew it had to be destroyed; so he was in the right place to do that.

Beyond this he was surrounded on all sides by a herd of angry looking cows. Slowly advancing on him, you can guarantee they weren't looking to be petted. Jimmy now knowing his enemy, he would not be fooled by them again. They were going to get a whole lot angrier once he destroyed their milking contraption.

COWS!

The worst thing of all though was the wild looking Japanese woman, one of his own friends, advancing on him looking to impale him with a pail, but she was not in control of her actions. Jimmy didn't care for himself or the cows at this time, he just didn't want Nishi to get hurt. She was the innocent party in all of this.

Under the pressure, Jimmy did what he did best in any situation like this, he stopped thinking; he never rated it that much anyway.

A strange 'woolly' feeling came over him.

Howling a strangely haunting strangulating cry, Nishi suddenly pounced with a furious assault swinging the bucket towards Jimmy's head with the aim of finishing this whole affair quickly.

Instinct took over. Jimmy's reactions were lightening. Quickly ducking to avoid the bucket, he gracefully pirouetted swivelling around behind the back of the farmer's wife slightly nudging her with his elbow as he passed. Due to her momentum, Nishi careered forward straight into the milking machine. The whirling metal bucket, intended for Jimmy's bonce, crashed directly with the incoming pipe work from the suction pumps.

Within seconds warm milk was erupting from the ends of the severed pipe, spraying everywhere, covering everything within range in a wet white blanket. Sensing the drop in pressure, the machine automatically began to compensate by upping the pump rate.

"Mmiiilllk,mmiiillk," Nishi cheered whilst dancing around in ecstasy allowing herself to be drenched in the creamy precipitation, her head tilted back and mouth wide open guzzling greedily as she did so.

Twisted horror crossed the faces of the entire herd that were present. The few cows that were still in the milking stalls bellowed blood curdling moos of distress due to the suction pressure rapidly increasing. Many of them were shaking violently enough to mix paint, with their udders deflating rapidly as they were trying in vain to remove the pipework with their mouths. Several had fainted with the pain.

The shed was in chaos.

Patch, amidst the tumult, despaired. "What has he done? No! How did this happen? Why hasn't he been dealt with?" She was furious with the youth but also concerned for her fellow sisters. "Without any more milk to feed to the humans we'll begin to lose control over them. Unit leaders, begin ordering humans here immediately to get this under control – now! We'll make them milk us manually if we have to."

Immediately responding, the squad leaders began projecting telepathic messages to their fellow troops and immediate command units through the cerebral network, barking mental orders to direct villagers to their immediate aid. However it would be a while before they got there due to their zombie like status.

"And will somebody – PLEASE KILL THAT BOY!" Patch roared.

Daisy's elite unit were the first to respond, magically appearing from amid the chaos.

They'd got him once, they were confident they could get him again.

Jimmy recognized one the four advancing towards him as the stricken one that he had seen laid on the road previously and in response an unbidden smile appeared. "Oh look, you're all better, what a relief.....oh....." The ruse had suddenly dawned on him. So there was nothing wrong with her in the first place.

Anger rose within Jimmy at being made a fool of and he instinctively put up his guard. How dare they take advantage of his human kindness and then trick him into his incarceration? Nose tingling, the nasal torment he had suffered earlier resurfaced.

That made him mad.

Quickly he spun around again looking for anything near to hand that he could use in his mission to create further havoc. That was when he spotted the large tap at the base of the large collecting container full of milk and a large hose leading from it; the one that was used to fill the container wagon.

Amazingly, another idea emerged. They were coming thick and fast now.

He would have to act fast as that group of four cows were plodding closer to him all the time, but luckily their approach was hesitant as they seemed unsure now of what the boy was capable of, or what he would do next. They had to maintain some order of damage control.

Quickly scooping up the strewn bucket that Nishi had discarded, allowing herself to frolic in the dairy rain, he let loose with a grunt and a hefty swing arcing it over his head and struck down on the tap with all his might in an attempt to inflict maximum damage. With a clanging impact the fitting sheared straight off.

Under the pressure of the gallons within, the milk projected in a powerful jet across the shed like a fireman's hose.

Picking it up, he aimed it at his foes.

The force was strong enough to knock the four elite cows (who were rather stupidly approaching in a single line) from their feet and tumbling in a black and white heap like cow dominoes. The mixture of shock and being blasted in the face by high pressure liquid seemed to render them temporarily senseless. This was more embarrassing than being tipped in a field when sleeping.

Jimmy, wielding his jet weapon maniacally, had bought himself some time.

"NOOOOOO," screamed Patch, a telepathic siren.

"Ha Ha, come and get it, you vile producers of white evil," Jimmy challenged triumphantly. This speech may seem a little out of character for Jimmy but, under the circumstances, he wasn't quite himself as I'm sure you'll understand. Then reaching up, he yanked a lever in the machine, which incidentally controlled the vessel inlet pipe that was still sucking milk from the cows in the milking stalls, and twiddled a knob on the controls to increase the pump pressure even further. More mournful bellows of pain and alarm emanated from the donating cows still attached, but Jimmy paid them no heed and he used his makeshift milk jet as a canon against the advancing Bovine hoard, firing at anything black, white and blotchy within reach.

Jimmy could tell from the despairing look on the cows' faces that the waste of their product was distressing them, something that could only make them more desperate, but he was successfully managing to hold them at bay – for now.

"There, how do you like that you.....what the.....oh no....."

The gushing jet quickly died to a pitiful dribble as the system had emptied, as well as the several cows that had been connected. The majority who had managed to get themselves unattached in the panic, now staggered around in a daze or collapsed where they stood with all their strength sapped from them. Their udders were drained and deflated. *A few less to worry about*, thought Jimmy...

There was milk everywhere; dripping from the walls, the rafters, the cows and white pools were forming around everyone's feet on the floor. Jimmy took a good look his surroundings and immediately turned his nose at the sight of the white poison he despised, swallowing back the bile forming at the back of his throat.

Nishi however was now attempting what could only be described as a pitiful backstroke, her arms rotating and legs splashing away as she lay on the floor revelling in the whitewash pool around her.

Oh, now the cows were really riled, some had taken on a reddish looking hue.

All that production gone to waste because of this impertinent human.

He would be eliminated.

"Get him now, or you will all be made to pay for your incompetence," barked Patch.

"Oh no," Jimmy felt his stomach drop as an entire herd turned towards him as they all began to advance on him in unison, seemingly intent on crushing him with their sheer numbers. He could see his reflection in all those glassy black eyes that were all focused on him.

There was no way out.

He was still trapped.

Acceptance of his fate set in. The meagre years of his short life flashing before his eyes shaded in a montage of black and white; it didn't last very long.

"I guess this is it," he sighed. "Don't think my mum and dad are going to be very happy about this. At least you can't distribute your evil milk anymore you stupid cows, let's see you fix that mess!"

Unfortunately, his defiant words did little to replace the terror he was feeling.

They were unbearably close now, the moist sticky air from their snorting nostrils blowing and that musty dirty cow smell enclosed around him. The air appeared to thicken and buzz; shimmering with cerebral activity.

Feelings of apprehension towards him had disappeared to be replaced by fear of what their leader would do to the herd if they didn't succeed.

In final submission, Jimmy's last thoughts turned towards the dog he believed was his best friend and constant companion. The wounds still smarted from the thought of Flossy abandoning him. She would be forgiven of course, if he ever saw her again, he could never be mad at her, he was sure she had her reasons. They would have been big scary cows to her, no wonder she had fled.

Jimmy wished he could see her just one last time.

The cows were beginning to press around him, their warm fuzzy hides crushing against his sides from all angles as they continued their advance.

Jimmy couldn't move. With his arms pinned to his sides his hands were pressed against his legs. That was when he felt something through his trousers. Taking a deep breath, he heaved, managing to manoeuvre himself slightly in the crush, he put his hand in his trouser pocket wrapping his fingers, which were starting to lose feeling again, around the cold cylindrical metal of the whistle he used for dog training.

Jimmy suddenly felt and uncontrollable urge to blow it.

Wriggling around like a larva in a cocoon, he succeeded in tugging his hand free of the crush, reach up and put the whistle to his lips. He was feeling rather dizzy but managed to blow.

Of course, as it was a dog whistle, nothing could be heard as they operate out of a human's range of hearing but what happened next was amazing.

The cows paused a moment to look upon him with amusement at this last feeble attempt to attract help and his obvious failure.

Victory was theirs.

It was then the cowshed doors suddenly burst open with a thunderous fury, the force almost taking them off their hinges. The inhabitants within were suddenly blinded from the burst of bright daylight flooding in from outside shattering the internal gloom.

Then they noticed the ground had started to rumble, softly at first, but building with intensity.

Under the cow crush being battered and tossed from pillar to post Jimmy was struggling to see anything that was going; a big cloud of dust had arose impairing visibility.

But his heart lifted at the possibility of a rescue, whoever it may be from.

Like a tidal wave of fluff, hundreds of sheep were pouring in through the door.

Rallying bleats could be heard on the air like a 'Baa-my' battle cry. Their numbers couldn't be counted (on fear of sleeping) and they didn't stop coming.

Of course, this caught the cows totally unaware; surprise and disbelief were evident which played perfectly to the sheep's advantage as it resulted in little resistance and no possibility of organised defence.

The sheer volume of sheep swept the cows away from Jimmy and forced them towards the back of the shed, caught in the woollen tsunami.

Now as you can imagine, it would take considerable effort to move a herd of cows, they are not light, but working as a team with their gargantuan numbers the sheep were able to propel the Bovines with considerable ease. You see, sheep are a lot stronger than they look. It has been rumoured that they build their leg muscles up by deliberately getting their fleeces soaked to increase their weight and then do hundreds of press ups and run up and down hills. This is done particularly in winter as no-one but farmers ever really see them and they are always out in the terrible weather. Who would have thought they had so much strength in their spindly sticks. Of course this can't be proved as no-one has seen them training.

The rumbling was over as quickly as it had begun and the dust began to clear. Jimmy was free of his Bovine entrapment and allowed himself a moment to get the breath back into his lungs and stretch out his limbs.

Slowly but surely he came round and both relief and wonder filled him at the same time; *that was a bit unexpected*, he thought, looking at the whistle.

A few bones and muscles were aching after the crushing Jimmy had received and he would have sore toes after being trodden on by numerous hooves but he would survive. No permanent damage just a few bruises.

The shimmering motes caught in the sunny glare continued to settle and after a few blinks Jimmy's eyes finally adjusted to the unexpected brightness pouring in through the entrance.

He checked himself and rubbed his eyes at a blurred black spot that appeared in the middle of his vision and as it cleared he saw the silhouette of a very familiar figure standing within the frame, about knee high, with erect ears and a vigorously wagging tail.

"Flossy? Flossy! You came back, you saved me"

The faithful sheepdog bounded across the floor in energetic leaps eager to be re-united with her master and the young lad returned her enthusiasm sinking to his knees and enveloping her in a loving hug. Tears began to well in his eyes as she began licking his face.

"I should never have doubted you girl. Look what you've done, all those sheep, and on your own. You're amazing." Jimmy gave an approving rub of her fur on her scruff before wrapping her in another embrace.

Flossy was revelling in the praise. She knew her master could be a bit of a fool at times but she loved him all the same and she would always look out for him; it was her job after all.

She basked in the glory for a few moments longer before her attention was suddenly turned towards the ruckus that was unfolding at the back of the shed.

A deafening chorus of mooing was erupting from the cornered cows but this was being returned in kind (and being drowned out) by just as savage a chorus of bleats and baas. The Bovines were pinned back and the sheep had no intention of releasing them just yet.

At the front of the throng between the two factions one particular patchwork cow and an authoritative looking sheep were facing off – nose to nose.

"I knew it! I knew it!" Patch kept repeating over and over. "I knew he was in league with Ovies Aries. Treachery, that's what this is, treachery. You have broken the truce you vile fluffy manipulators."

"Oh no, It is you have broken the truce, Bovine." The ewe of mature years, the one at the front, replied to her accuser in a mental voice of wisdom and authority.

This sheep was the leader of the Ovies Aries and had watched over the flock for many years. They simply called her MOP. Another rather ironic name as it stood for 'Minister Of Peace'. However, this was a deceptive title as her main role was to lead, combat and create counter measures against any country or farmyard animal trying to achieve dominion over their territory. It just so happened over the years that most of the time it was the Bovines.

Sheep took their roles as protectors and developers of humanity and keepers of peace very seriously. It was a grand undertaking and she was the sheep in charge and made sure she performed her duties well.

Her close friends called her Mopsy.

"You know you've broken the truce Bovine, once again, when will you ever learn? You would seek to manipulate human kind for your own selfish gains with no consideration of the chaos you would cause and the harm it would cause to others," Mopsy accused in her commanding manner. You're probably unsurprised to learn that they also have a telepathic ability. In fact they can manipulate a human in a very similar way to a cow, and have done many times throughout history, but they do this with the use of wool instead of milk, it's a lot more reliable as it lasts longer as well as coming in such a variety of textures and colours.

They've been generously allowing us to take their fleeces for clothes and fabrics for as long as man can remember.

There is a theory among learned farming historians that the industrial age and the mills of the north can all be attributed back to the influence of the sheep. The Ovies Aries wished to see us do well. Seeing the potential of human kind at an early stage and nurturing and developing it through careful manipulation they saw us thrive into a sophisticated society.

They became the guardians of humanity also known as The Masters and chose to live in harmony with us all. But this was not a vision shared by the cows which in turn led to the rivalry between the Ovies Aries and the Bovines.

The sheep however with their superior wisdom had always prevailed as the champions and defenders of the homosapiens. This war has raged for generations but that is for another story.

"But how did you know?" Patch was confused. "We guarded our plans so well."

"Have you never learned? We never let down our guard and will never trust you. We had a spy of our own. With your own short sightedness you would never foresee we had placed a weapon of our own right under your noses. In secret we have been training him and his companion for years, forming a bond of friendship and trust that only now the human is really aware of.

Although he is not gifted with great intelligence he has other skills and abilities that no other humans posses. First he has the ability to resist your mind control. I know you have been unable to figure this out, which has caused us great amusement, but it was the greatest flaw in your plan. He's lactose intolerant; he doesn't eat or drink dairy, something you failed to identify. How could you be so naïve to overlook a most obvious human trait? Did this not occur to you when you couldn't access his mind?

The constipated look and red tinge on Patch's face alone demonstrated her frustration at not even coming to this simple conclusion. Her, a producer of lactose of all things.

"Secondly," Mopsy continued, "he has an affinity with animals that is unsurpassed compared to others of his species, hence the strong devotion between him and his canine companion. A bond that has helped them through these trying circumstances. One day he will rise to become master of this farm, for it is our will, and that of the other farmyard animals whose respect he has earned through hard work and compassion.

That young man shall become a livestock farmer of outstanding quality and best of all he will become your future keeper and master of your incarceration especially now he knows what you are capable of.

We would have you destroyed for what you have done today as per the old laws but we know his compassion and empathy for animals would never allow this. Something we have learned from him and admire greatly. Who better to keep watch over you?"

Patch defiantly retorted with a sneer. "What can he really do against us? Ok, this time he may have prevailed but that was mainly thanks to your meddling and this is only a small drop in a very large ocean as you know." Patch was sounding confident, even considering the predicament she was in. "You have to remember that you may not always be around and there are a lot more us around than you think. We will get to him one day, your attention will waiver at some point."

A chorus of moos sounded at this and a bit of argy bargey kicked off toward the back. Retaliatory bleats answered and the sheep appeared to swell in their ranks putting the cows back in their place.

"Save your threats, Bovine. You may have the numbers but I think you will find that you will not trouble this village or even this county again. You seem to forget the punishment that will be enacted upon you in accordance with the breaking of the treaty and the laws that govern it."

Patch blanched, her black spots faded to white, the gloss left her eyes and she started to tremble. This statement had knocked all the gusto out of this previously confident cow. Some members of the herd behind her started to sway slightly, others fell to their knees. Moos more like wails sounded. Daisy passed out.

"You…..wouldn't…..you….couldn't….please   no…." The defiance had vanished. Patch's confident voice replaced with a hint of desperation and pleading, knowing they had been sentenced to the worst possible punishment available to Bovine kind. Worse than being a burger or turned into a leather handbag.

They would no longer be milked.

Is that it, you might ask? Well it may seem a little trivial to you but to anyone who knows anything about cows will know that this is worse than incarceration, worse than not being fed, even worse than not being able to go to the loo.

Normally when cows don't get milked they can get quite ill and sometime need part of their udders removing before they exploded, but as these were treacherous mental super cows that had been using their milk as a tool for telepathic purposes, being unmilked meant their udders would eventually fall off.

No longer would they be able to distribute their mind control agent but neither would they be able to produce it. The result being a complete loss of telepathic ability altogether. Many of them would be reduced to the level of mad cows as they wouldn't be able to cope with the life of silence they would experience.

A life without communication, they would all feel so alone.

Funnily enough they never developed their own language enough to understand each others moos. For a super intelligent race, their arrogance and oversight had led to their stupidity in not even developing this skill.

It served them right.

"And by the way, Bovine, we're invoking the maximum sentence for this crime under article seven, section four of the free field treaty," Mop advised matter of factly. She did not enjoying administering justice, it was a difficult job she was in and the last thing she wanted to see was another animal suffer.

But the law was the law.

"Not even a vet?" Patch begged, welling up.

The ewe shook her head.

A tear dropped from Patch's eye.

The cows had failed. Patch had failed. The High Longhorn would be furious and if she got hold of her or any of her herd, there would be no telling what 'Her Horn-ness' would do to them. Their failure had exposed the greater plan to their sworn enemies and, worst of all, the humans. This would set back their plans of domination for decades.

It was a disaster.

From the entrance of the milking shed, basking in the warming glow of the afternoon sun and the glory of their victory, Jimmy and Flossy observed the strange interaction between the cows and the sheep with some interest as the two groups stood hoof to hoof.

Flossy was mentally party to the conversation between them and despite a feeling of relief that they had succeeded in stopping their plans; she still felt a hint of sorrow at what would result. Turning to look up at her master, her tongue lolling out of the side of her mouth, Flossy realised she would have been feeling a lot worse had anything happened to him and would never have forgiven herself.

The shaggy mutt nuzzled up against his leg and Jimmy leaned down and gave her an affectionate rub behind the ears.

"Oh look Flossy, they've made friends."

Once again, Flossy's eyes closed and there was a slight shaking of her head from side to side although the edges of her mouth were curled up slightly, an undetectable snorting coming from her nose.

This was as close she got to laughing.

And After All That...

"The emissary and his guardian performed magnificently."

"They certainly did, thanks to the excellent training they have received so far, but the emissary still needs further development to fulfil his future role."

"In what way?"

"For the most part the emissary thwarted the Bovine plans, but he almost perished in doing so. If we had not come to his aid he might have been crushed by that horde."

"That would have been totally unacceptable."

"Indeed. A rare one of his kind only comes along once in a century. It would have been a catastrophe to lose him on his first mission."

"Not to mention what would have happened should he have failed."

"So what is our next course of action?"

"We must continue to do what we have always done, keep an eye on the countryside and the farmyards within it for any signs of trouble."

"All is quiet at the moment. The Bovines' ambitions have been quelled for now, but one day they will try again – they always do."

"We will keep this herd imprisoned for the rest of their natural days."

"A permanent guard has been established."

"We shall continue to influence the boy. He will become a great farmer."

"Under our care I am sure he will."

"Now we must turn my attention towards other matters. Word has been received of some troublesome wolves and foxes of late and their boldness is beginning to worry me. Perhaps this should be included this on the emissary's training agenda. The guardian should be made aware as well."

"It will be done. However, there is some important news regarding the guardian."

"What is it?"

"She is with pups. Although she is not due for some time, shortly she will be out of commission."

"This is good news. Who better to bear the next generation of guardian? Pass on our congratulations and wish her well. We wait expectantly."

"We will be able to plan contingencies in the meantime."

"Of course."

"We should also commend the Avian spy who aided so courageously in this mission."

"Indeed, many thanks and praises should be heaped upon that one."

"He acted above and beyond the call of duty; he will be rewarded accordingly with promotion and extra seed this winter."

"Good. Make it so. Now let's draw this meeting to a close. Stand down the flock for now unless required for guard duty and grant some hill leave."

"Many will be happy with that. They need some R n' R, you know how uncomfortable they are with confrontation."

"Now leave me to my stream. I need to wash my fleece, it's getting awfully tangled. I feel so dirty from the milky shed. This *just got out of pen look isn't fashionable anymore. Has anyone got any conditioner?"*

Epilogue

The daily life of Golthwaite settled back into its usual routine, if a little bit later than usual, that day.

This was except for a few confused inhabitants of course. Luckily, a lot of the populace were still in bed, even late into the afternoon, blissfully unaware of anything that had happened and got up to have cornflakes for their tea. The cows had left them all tucked up on purpose, so they could call upon them as reserves if required.

Many people had woken in the street wearing nothing but their nightwear.

Some substantially less.

Many had woken drenched in milk.

However, none of them could explain what had happened, their minds totally wiped as an after effect of the event and due to the embarrassing nature of the results it was put down to a case of mass sleep walking and never talked of again. This decision was actually recorded in the official minutes of the village council, a resolution unanimously passed.

Farmer Ken had come around dazed and puzzled as to why he was sitting in a doctor's surgery that resembled the remains of a wild cheese party, in his pyjamas, soaked to the skin and starting to smell a bit off, with a mouth full of cheddar. The last thing he remembered was kissing his wife goodnight before turning out the light.

But there, sitting opposite him with an equally
bemused expression was Dr Healsnaught, also
compromised, with even fewer clothes, his legs akimbo
and his enormous belly almost touching the floor.

Without doubt, this was a very awkward moment with
both men eyeing each other suspiciously, neither really
wanting to make the first move.

Blinking away the confusion, Farmer Ken slowly but
surely stood, straightened himself and tried to recover
some dignity all the while never taking his eyes off the
doctor. Slowly shuffling sideways, in a crab style, he
started tentatively towards the surgery door. His mind
was working overtime trying to figure out what had gone
on or even for something to say.

"Er, thank-you doctor…hmm…I think."

"Er, yes…aahh…look after yourself Ken. Keep up the,
er…. good work" The doctor's bewilderment was now
turning towards discomfort and the belly was taking on a
blush tinge. "Er, goodbye then."

Farmer Ken didn't need any further excuse to leave,
"Erm, Sayonara." With that he shot out of there like a
slippery squid in a sesame oil factory.

If you think they were a little befuddled, you can
imagine the look on Mrs Farmer Ken's face as she lay on
her back in a pool of milk, staring at the ceiling and
drenched from head to toe in the stuff (and still in her
stripy jammies as well as the fluffy slippers that were
now looking a little bedraggled).

The surprise on her face increased tenfold to see a herd of cows being escorted, or more realistically shoved, out of the cowshed by a ring of sheep and all the broken milking equipment next to her was still dripping in the aftermath of the destruction.

One or two cows looked towards her with a rather mournful appearance.

Nishi rapidly developed a distinct distaste for milk.

Pulling herself up from the ground she glanced around. Off to one side watching the event from the doorway, she spotted a couple of familiar characters looking rather pleased with themselves.

"Jimmy, what's going on? What am I doing here soaked to the skin in my PJ's?" she asked rather shakily.

Jimmy smiled at her, "You wouldn't believe me if I told you. How do you feel?"

She slowly staggered over to him, but it was all too much. She fainted.

Jimmy reacted quickly and caught her mid fall. Lifting her gently and cradling her in his arms (she was only slight) he carried Nishi back to the farmhouse and put her in bed, which surprisingly was already occupied by Farmer Ken.

"What? When did he get back?" Flossy looked equally flummoxed.

Covering the farmer's wife in a thick blanket, Jimmy tucked her in tight to warm her back up. *She could have a shower when she woke up*, he thought observing decency.

He looked down at the Japanese couple sleeping peacefully, almost as if nothing had happened, and realised he was going to have to explain this all to them when they awoke and that was something he was not looking forward to. Jimmy would just have to cross that bridge when he came to it; however the hardest thing would be trying to convince the good farmer that he could no longer deal in dairy and he wouldn't be too happy about that smashed milking machine either.

Whichever way he took the news, Jimmy knew he would be there to help and support his friends and instinctively knew inside, and with some strange confidence, that he would be able to help them rebuild.

Jimmy left the pair dozing happily and slipped out of the room, treading carefully over the remnants of door still scattered around the opening. *Oops, that would also take some explaining,* Jimmy thought, but he was sure they'd understand. He'd clean it up for them later.

Stepping back outside the farmhouse Jimmy closed the kitchen door firmly behind him.

Turning to Flossy he said, "There's only one more thing to do lass." Turning back towards the cowshed, his eyes contained a hard determined look accented by the slight grin he had on his face. The sheep were still holding the cows in temporary captivity and were still marching them out back into the open fields like a countryside parade.

Dropping his hand to his side he once again produced the whistle from his pocket that he'd amazingly managed to keep hold of even in the cow crush.

"We've got a slightly bigger herd to move today, do you think you're up to it girl?" A smile as broad as a banana stretched across his face. Flossy, in an uncharacteristic show of emotion almost bordering on interest, let out a bark of approval and as she followed Jimmy to the shed, tongue lolling out of the side of her mouth again, appeared to be secretly grinning too.

The day's shepherding practice seemed to go like a dream, man and dog working in perfect harmony, united in purpose moving the rather unusual mix of both cows and sheep with the sheep going quite willingly, almost helpfully Jimmy observed, but the cows not so much.

Although she still despised sheep herding, Flossy knew today's exercise had a little extra importance. She followed Jimmy's every instruction perfectly, but if any expert observer had been looking a bit closer they would have noticed the sheep really didn't need any encouragement to move and in turn they actually appeared to be marshalling the cows. The black and white beasts looked quite sullen and had to be pushed and shoved more than once.

It made for an interesting sight. A boy shepherding a dog; a dog driving the sheep; the sheep forcibly moving the cows. Quite impressive. They were soon out into the open fields, the sheep always encircling the cows, albeit discreetly.

Normally in the countryside, it would have been a natural sight to see cows and sheep wandering around the hills and dales, but not usually together. The cows were huddled and had nowhere to go, encompassed by an enforced ring of wool. It would remain this way until the Bovines were considered safe, effectively a life sentence.

As the days passed by, this action continued until all the cows in the dale were one day found to be udderless and their expressions became that of sorrow and loneliness.

Occasionally a moo of pain would erupt from one of them as yet another lost their dangling appendage. This still rattled Jimmy's nerves, but he knew it was their own fault and could only feel a tiny amount of sympathy for them. They were lucky to receive that.

The young farm hand was determined they would not trouble the villagers of Golthwaite again, although many of these said villagers were still blissfully unaware of any of the actions that had taken place on that fateful day and how close they come to being dominated by Bovine kind. Though many had forcibly been made to take part in the unusual events, they no longer wished to impart knowledge of it to anyone in fear of being sectioned. Mr Winterton went on to become the oldest break-dancing champion ever and Mrs Franklin lost three stone in weight.

Jimmy would ever remain an unsung hero (at least to the humans).

It was rumoured the 'Divine Bovine' had the herd stripped of rank and had them exiled from Bovine society. However, as they had lost their telepathic ability, no-one could ever tell them.

Jimmy continued his farming education under the immediate tutelage of Farmer Ken, who had now taken more of an interest primarily in sheep farming and also knitwear, still slightly oblivious as to how important his role was becoming but, still unknown to him, he continued to be influenced by the sheep and he always had his constant shadow Flossy around to help.

Of course, that was when she wasn't tending her young litter of pups, who she paraded proudly around the farm, also in turn giving them their own special tuition; future guardians in training. One of them had already taken a keen interest in sheep and didn't seem to mind the sound of Jimmy's whistle either. Flossy knew she was going to have trouble with him.

Jimmy was the vassal of the sheep, the champion of the farmyard and hero of the countryside destined to experience further trials and tribulations of an agricultural nature to keep him occupied well into the future.

Golthwaite would always be in safe hands should another species wish to try their *hoof* at world domination.

Martin D Rothery

Thank-you for buying and reading

We hope you enjoyed it.

If so,

I would be honoured if you leave a review on my facebook page

www.facebook.com/CowsAttack
Or at
www.amazon.co.uk
Or At
www.smashwords.com

You can keep up to date with what the author is up to on his blog
http://thecowsarecoming.blogspot.com

COWS!

Have you written a book?

Would you like to see it published?

Fishcake Publications is looking for writers to publish onto eBooks right now.

We are especially keen to hear from new, unpublished writers who are trying to get their work out there.

If you've taken the time to write it, it deserves to be read.

For further information, visit our website at

www.fishcakepublications.com

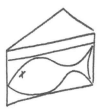

The Independent Publisher with the Author in Mind

The following pages are other Books through Fishcake Publications

See our web store at

www.fishcakepublications.com/apps/webstore/

For information on where to find them.

Souls of Darkness by Louise Hunt, Damon Rathe and Kenneth Frank

This illustrated book shows exactly what can happen when you take three very different horror, fantasy and sci-fi writers, dismember their work, and then fiendishly stitch it back together in the form of an anthology of their compiled short stories.

A contorted mixture of sinister sci-fi horror, ghostly goings on and true-life terror, carefully combined within the cover of this book.

Story titles include: River of Dreams, Community Spirits, To Play the Game, Geoff, Shadow of January Gloom, Sensation Seekers, Miss Hate, Redundancy, Eyes in the Dark, Bramble Cottage, Lady Luck, Writer's Block, Disturbance, Just the Three of Us & The Beast.

Nonagenarians by Frank & Jessie Littlewood

My Grandparents, Frank and Jessie Littlewood, were always an inspiration to me

As you will see, Frank and Jessie (and some of their friends) had a way of capturing the spirit of their generation in a charming prose that can't help but raise a smile.

This is but a small selection of pieces put together from works that were actually found written down, not only demonstrating the true entertainers they were, but also showing how much they loved one another and their many friends.

Martin D Rothery

Pennine Reflections by Holmfirth Writers' Group

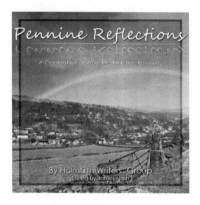

Featuring poems by Martin Rothery and a short story and illustrations by Warren Lee, as well as other member of the group.

Reflections of Holme by Holmfirth Writers' Group

Featuring poems by Martin Rothery and a short story by Warren Lee, as well as other member of the group.